The Lights Go Out in Lychford

THE LIGHTS GO OUT IN LYCHFORD

PAUL CORNELL

A TOM DOHERTY ASSOCIATES BOOK

NEW YORK

This is a work of fiction. All of the characters, organizations, and events portrayed in this novella are either products of the author's imagination or are used fictitiously.

THE LIGHTS GO OUT IN LYCHFORD

Copyright © 2019 by Paul Cornell

Cover photograph © Hans Neleman/Getty Images
Cover design by Fort

Edited by Lee Harris

A Tor.com Book
Published by Tom Doherty Associates
120 Broadway
New York, NY 10271

www.tor.com

Tor® is a registered trademark of
Macmillan Publishing Group, LLC.

ISBN 978-1-250-24946-3 (ebook)
ISBN 978-1-250-24947-0 (trade paperback)

First Edition: November 2019

For Lizbeth Myles

The Lights Go Out in Lychford

1

THE AIR CONTAINED THE first chill of autumn. Judith Mawson knew it well. She was walking along the side of the playing field, by the allotments, carrying a bag. She didn't know what she was doing here. She stopped. She *had* known. She patted herself down. She was in her light coat, and too cold, but she was always too cold. Her handkerchief was . . . where was it? Oh, tucked in her cuff. Where she never kept it. Probably.

Right. She must have come out here for some reason. She looked out over the playing fields and watched parents and children on the swings and slides. What day was it? No idea. How could she find out what she was doing here? Ah. The bag. She looked in it. It contained a sheaf of posters, a box of drawing pins and a packet of Blu Tack. She picked out one of the posters: *Lychford Festival. Bands, beer tent, fun run, children's shows. A great day out for the whole family!*

Well, that sounded hellish.

She looked around, and saw, ahead of her, a notice-board. Ah. Right. Got it. Someone must have signed her up for this. They must have realised how helpless she was feeling right now. Oh, give the old bugger summat to do, keep her busy, that's what they were thinking, when everyone in this town owed their lives to her, several times over.

Oh. She'd just remembered a lot of things about who she was and what she did. And a lot of it was pretty damn surprising. She was the wise woman, the hedge witch, who'd bathed in the waters of the well in the woods decades ago and had spent her days since protecting Lychford from the evil (or just very different in a probably evil sort of way) stuff beyond its invisible borders. But now those borders were basically gone, because her apprentice, Autumn, had made some big errors of judgment.

Not the girl's fault. Judith's fault for not knowing what to do with an apprentice. She'd known she needed one because . . . because this forgetting had been going on a lot longer than she'd told people.

Where had her power gone? Where had her knowledge gone? Into the forgetting. Into the bloody past. Ever since they'd gone to rescue those idiots who'd strayed into the other worlds that surrounded Lychford. That had been too much for her, in the end. She'd carried the magic of this town on her back too long. If summat big did come out of the darkness for them now, with the boundaries only makeshift replacements, did she have anything at all left in her to help? She was pretty sure she were all right at the moment, as she stared at this bloody noticeboard, but she was pretty sure she was okay most of the time. Then she'd find evidence that someone had been walking around in her body being stupid while she was away in cloud cuckoo land. And that weren't magic, that were just this useless porridge between her ears, going off. She'd gone around the bingo the other night, sitting down at tables where she didn't know anyone, asking where her sister was, that was what her son . . . whatever he were called . . . that was what he'd told her. She couldn't believe she'd been there. She'd yelled at him. Of course she bloody had.

Postering. That was what she was doing now.

She shouldn't yell at him. At Shaun—that was his name. She should do what Lizzie and Autumn said, because they were the only ones she had now, the only ones who could understand enough to help her. That must be why she was here at this bloody noticeboard, because she'd finally got to the point in her life where she'd do things for whoever asked because she were desperate.

Didn't deserve help. Not after the life she'd had.

Oh God, she was frightened. She was more scared of this than of anything she'd faced down in the dark of the woods across all those years.

Come on, you stupid woman. Look at this board. Do the job. What have you got here? Every inch of the noticeboard was taken up with posters and postcards: film shows at the Fincham Hall; yoga classes; the History Society had a talk about the Civil War; baby bounce at the library; the festival in the next town, Northcott. She recalled now that she'd seen several of these posters on the previous noticeboards she'd visited. *Well done, brain, good effort, dear.* Were any of these past their sell-by date? She realised she had no idea what day it was. She looked again at the poster she was meant to put up. It looked to be the final version, with all the attractions on it. The Festival was in mid-September. She looked again in her bag and saw that she'd bought the *Gazette.* Or found it. If this was the current one, it was the week of September 3rd, which meant . . . no, all of these events on the posters were still to come.

So. What to do?

Well, the History Society seemed to get everywhere. They laminated their posters and stapled them to posts. They wouldn't miss one or two. Judith pulled out the bolts from the noticeboard, swung back the double glass doors, took the poster down, crumpled it up, and put it in her pocket. There still wasn't room to put up hers, though. Bloody Northcott had no business putting up posters for their festival in Lychford. It wasn't like the

Lychford Festival went over there and . . . well, they might, Judith had no idea. But whatever . . . down it came. Still not quite enough room. The last person who'd postered here had arranged everything that was left with fiendish precision. The film show at the hall was summat by Agatha Christie, and Judith hated Agatha Christie, so . . . Finally, she had space to pin up the Festival poster. She did so, and triumphantly swung the doors closed again.

Her Festival poster was now half obliterated by the wooden edges of each of the glass doors where they met in the middle.

Judith glared at the noticeboard. She'd had no idea this job was going to be so bloody awkward. This didn't seem like anything she'd normally be getting up to. Normally she'd be on those swings over there with her mum and dad. Where had they got to? Well, of course they'd be at home, wouldn't they?

What? Of course *not*. Where had that come from? No, couldn't think about that, didn't make sense. She turned and looked over to the playing fields. They weren't there. She could see the old cottages that had stood there, one of them falling into the others, where its thatched roof had burned. Marie Higgs had lived there, and Alex Sarll, who'd left to go into the merchant navy. After she'd finished here, she'd go and knock on his door and see if he could come out to play.

She realised there was a weight behind her, an odd sort of weight. No, come on, not an odd sort of weight at all—it was the kind of feeling she'd become used to, being the wise woman of Lychford all these years.

All what years? No, no, had someone said summat? What had she been thinking about?

Here, this was an *urgent* weight. It said there might be danger. Or opportunity. She turned to see. There was a path that led across the allotments, right over two of them, in fact. It had high hedges on both sides. It turned a sharp corner. It was lit by a different sun than was in the sky on this late summer day. A sad sun. An awful sun. The sort of sun that you got after a fire. The smell that went with it was the smell of approaching winter. The path didn't seem to be in this world at all. It weren't attached to anything. It was like one of her posters, one thing put on top of another. It had never been here, not as far as she knew.

"What's that?" she asked.

"It's new," said Doreen. Her sister was standing at the noticeboard with her. She had her hair like Doris Day and was wearing that blue-and-white striped dress she put on whenever they went down the hall for a dance.

"I thought 'twere," said Judith. She realised she'd finished her task. The poster was up now, and she could see all of it, even if the lettering was so small she couldn't read all of it. She looked around again, and the cottages, the new path, and her sister, were gone. Well, that was what magic was like, wasn't it? Probably. Where had the magic started and ended there? Where should she go now? Home, for a cup of tea. But where was that? Where were her parents?

If she kept walking, she decided, she would probably find what she was after.

———————

"Dementia," said Shaun Mawson. "Let's call it what is, Reverend."

The Reverend Lizzie Blackmore realised that she had indeed been euphemising, something she never did when it was her elderly parishioners who were suffering. "I'm sorry," she said.

"No, well, it's hard to face it, isn't it?" Shaun was still in his police uniform, sitting with a cup of tea at Lizzie's kitchen table in the Vicarage.

"That's why I wanted to talk to you about it. Apart from yourself, Autumn and I are the ones closest to your mum—"

"The only ones who'll talk to her, you mean." He smiled as he said it.

"—and we were wondering how you planned to proceed." Lizzie realised that, again, that wasn't as direct as she wanted to be. "I mean, do you have power of attorney for Judith?"

"As of last week. I went to see Pete at Stanshaw and Kemp, and got the papers together, and I took them over and had a sit-down with Mum. She nodded along and asked me to leave them with her so she could read them before she signed them. I didn't think she would, but when I came back, she had. I told her it was for the best, then she told me that now I could . . . do what I'd always wanted to do, put her away in a home and never have to see her again!" Shaun kept smiling, but his eyes didn't.

Lizzie closed her eyes. "I'm sorry. I hear that a lot from relatives in your position."

"Then a couple of minutes later she asked me if I'd found those papers she'd signed, then a couple of minutes after that she told me I should stop bringing those papers over, because she'd never sign them."

"So, do you think consent here is . . . complicated?"

"No. She signed them. It's sorted."

Lizzie wanted to say that she knew there was a lot more behind that typically concrete policeman's statement. But she didn't want to hurt Shaun by getting him to plumb depths he didn't want to explore. He was middle-aged and had never married. He was the sort who still enjoyed, when he wasn't doing his job, being one of the lads down the pub. He'd probably trundle along to the end of his life, just the same. He was probably thinking a lot about that now, thanks to his mum. They all were.

"I don't think," he continued, "we need to do this yet. She's still looking after herself okay. But she's forgetting more and more. I went 'round there the other day, and she had three dinners sitting in the oven. She'd made it for herself three times."

"And are you thinking about how long it might be before she forgets to switch something off?" Lizzie was pretty sure neither Shaun nor Judith's savings, if there were any, were enough for a home help.

"That had occurred to me. But I pop over every night to make sure she's okay. Like I said, it's not time yet."

"I'm sure you'll make the right choice. And we'll be here to help when you do."

"Thanks for that. There's a good retirement home in town. Ashdown House. I've had a look around in there, and it were a sheer relief—lots for them to do, a really good atmosphere. Though you do see ones who are just staring into space, or who are shouting. God, I didn't like to hear that shouting." He stopped and took a long drink. "Anyway, that's what I'm considering. If she went in there, it's not as if we'd all vanish from her life."

"Absolutely."

"Also," said Shaun, keeping his "just the facts, ma'am" voice going, "I've been worrying about . . . Mum always sort of . . . made out that what you two and she did was, like, important. That summat terrible might happen if she stopped. Is that where we are right now? How worried should I be?"

Lizzie considered, just for a moment, telling Shaun the truth. He had, after all, always known that his mum's involvement with magic was real. She decided swiftly against. What would be gained by panicking this man, the town's entire law enforcement community? She managed her most comforting smile. "You've got enough to worry about. Leave that side of it to me and Autumn."

———————

Autumn Blunstone stared through the mist above one of the beakers on her work table, and realised she was falling asleep. At 9 A.M. She'd had a few hours of slumber, somewhen in the early hours. She couldn't keep this going. Soon she'd be no good to anyone, and . . . well, she was no good to anyone now.

It was all her fault. She'd allowed an old, deep-seated anger out to play; she had let it out, and as a result, the barriers around the town—that had protected this nexus of worlds from everything that lay beyond, protected all of this reality, even—had collapsed. Judith, who, it turned out, had been mentoring Autumn with a view to her taking over, had, in her efforts to rescue people, used up almost all the energy she had. So in one move, Autumn had pulled down the walls and hobbled the guardian. All because she was angry at things she *should* be angry at. Damn it. She couldn't even feel the guilt for that straightforwardly.

In the weeks after, Judith had largely retreated to her cottage. She was still meant to be Autumn's employee, here at Witches, Autumn's magic shop. Autumn was still paying her, but when she did come in, the conversations they had weren't something she wanted customers to hear. She wanted Judith to keep as much of her dignity as possible, and the residents of Lychford, especially those who frequented her shop, did like to share the local news.

Not that she was opening the shop very often. She'd been spending her days, instead, on two projects. The first involved working her way through everything she could find—from what notes she'd made since accepting the reality of magic, and from the Internet—on sorcerous ways to combat the depredations of old age. She hadn't found anything she could use. The sunnier traditions of magic, when it came to illness, were all about treating symptoms, and wandered alarmingly toward the idea that nature should take its course. The darker side, of course, said that nothing was impossible, but that terms and conditions applied. And right now, given what might be immediately threatening Lychford, given the guilt Autumn felt already, she wasn't even tempted. After what little she'd learned from the first, her second project was becoming more urgent every day. If she couldn't restore Judith's marbles, she would have to step up and attempt to protect Lychford herself. With the aid of Lizzie, of course, but it wasn't as if there seemed to be any implicit need for the wise woman of the town to have helpers. She was supposed to be friends with the local vicar, and Judith had considered the idea of an apprentice, and had thus let the three of them become a thing, but the awful fact was that defending the town, and the rest of reality, was largely down to the wise woman herself.

It was becoming clear that the outsider would have to defend the town. Not that she'd truly seen herself as an outsider until the last few months. But maybe it had always been the case. She wasn't sure she'd ever known how to be wise. If only Judith had kept much in the way of records. But the trunks in her attic, when the old woman had allowed Autumn up there to search, had turned out to be filled with journals written in a truly impenetrable hand, a few twigs, which all felt like they'd once possessed magical power that was long gone, and several unidentifiable items that were actually rotting. It was as if the material memory of the wise woman was decaying just as her biological memory was. Maybe that wasn't a metaphor, even. That was where Autumn's science kept failing her, the idea that in magic metaphor was often reality. But the ... poetic connections ... between cause and effect that seemed to be the case in magic weren't chaotic, they were a system that could be learned, and so they weren't divorced from the scientific approach. There was just a step in the way. A step she kept tripping over. Which *was* actually a metaphor, just for once.

She realised she'd been on the edge of a dream. There was noise coming from somewhere. It was from the shop. Someone was knocking on the door. She heaved herself upright and went to answer it. The only thing that made her want to was the idea that it might be Judith. But no, it probably wasn't. These days she wasn't often out and about.

Autumn opened the front door to find herself face to face with her boyfriend, Luke. Well, she was pretty sure he was still her boyfriend. They hadn't actually spoken much in the last couple of weeks. "Hi," he said.

"Hi." She didn't want to give him the impression she really had to get back to what she was doing, but she wasn't sure she could help it.

"So . . . is everything okay?"

Autumn bit her lip. She hadn't told him anything about what had happened. Mainly because he didn't know magic was real. So, like the rest of the town, he was aware that she'd been questioned about a disappearance, and that the old man who'd disappeared had since come back to Lychford and wouldn't talk to anyone about where he'd been. There'd been a few jokes down the pub about that. They'd laughed about what she'd done to him, and her joining in had meant that they didn't believe she actually *had* done anything to him. Probably. Luke might not actually be so sure. She'd told him, as a cover story for the presence of magic in her life, that she had some mental health issues. That therefore Luke could expect her to sometimes say weird stuff and that people would sometimes say weird stuff to her in return. As cover stories went, it was pretty ridiculous. And harder on her, probably, than telling the truth would be. It had had the added effect of making Luke careful around her. And thus, though they'd come close a couple of times, Autumn hadn't had sex with him. And God, she really wanted to. When she had a minute. Or, rather, about a day to convince him she was in her right frame of mind and that her consent was enthusiastic.

"It's fine," she said now, lying.

"What is?"

"*I'm* fine."

"Can I come in?"

This was a bit like with the lads down the pub. If she said no now, it'd be a real indicator that all was not fine. She let him in. He reacted to the darkness and the smell of chemicals.

"Oh," he said. "Is this the house of a serial killer?"

"No!" She realised that had been a shout, which had genuinely startled him, both with its noise and its implications. She turned it into a cough. "I mean, sorry, I've been making stuff in the back, I've been really busy." She hadn't kissed him during this visit. They were at least usually doing that. She really should have already. But now the moment had kind of passed.

"Busy with what? Can I help?"

Which was when something went bang in Autumn's workroom. She jumped, looked over at the door. The bangs continued. Something was banging on the door between the shop front and her workshop in the back. She looked back to Luke.

"I think it wants to get out," he said.

Maybe he thought she owned a dog? "Oh, don't worry about that," she said. The bangs started to get faster.

"Autumn . . ." Luke began, "are you . . . ?"

"Yes?"

"Are you a dominatrix?"

She found she could laugh. "Oh, entirely the opposite. I mean," she quickly added, "I'm not in control of anything."

"So, are you going to tell me what that noise is?"

Autumn was actually quite afraid of that noise, because she had no idea what it could be. She marched, nevertheless, over to the door, her hand on the protective charms she now habitually kept in the back pocket of her jeans. She reached out with her magical senses through the door and found only a loud sense of her own presence. So whatever this was, it was something she'd made. Feeling slightly reassured, she opened the door.

Something flew past her, straight at Luke, and hit him in the crotch.

With a little agonised yelp, he fell forward.

She ran to him. He was wincing but didn't seem to be . . . whatever that would do to a bloke. Attached to his groin, or rather to his pocket, which must have saved him from some of the impact, was her incursion meter. She hadn't been able to think of a more mystical name for it. It was a pebble with a toy magnet stuck through it. She'd searched for an appropriate rock at a crossing point of three of the borders. She'd been hoping that, over the centuries, the rock had picked up a sense of . . . borderness. The magnet was to give it a sense of . . . magnetness. Magnetry. Not actually magnetism but the magical,

storybook version of that. She'd put it together as an ex-
periment to find out if she could detect whether or not
something had come into town across the slight, almost
gestural barriers they'd managed to put in place in lieu of
the real thing. Like a compass, it was supposed to point at
anything that had come over. She hadn't had time to test
it very much.

So, wait, did that mean that Luke was some sort of
occult threat? Was this even the real Luke? Or had just
his todger somehow been replaced by an evil duplicate?
Wow, how would that work?

"What the hell?" He tried to pull the pendant off him,
but it wouldn't budge. "Is it stuck in my—?" He pulled
the wallet from his pocket. The pendant leapt after it and
attached itself, pinning the billfold to the ground.

So, not Luke himself, but whatever was in that wallet.
There was something in there that had come through
the barriers. But before she could look into that, she had
some explaining to do.

"It's a magnet I've been working on," she said. "You
know. Magic. I mean stage magic. Children's parties." She
knew that Luke's understanding of what had just happened, given that he didn't share her magical senses,
might have been more prosaic. But how mundanely
could one experience a levitating rock attacking one's
nads?

"I didn't know you did that sort of magic. I thought you were all about New Age meditation stuff. But there's nothing in here that's metal..." He started pulling out his bank cards, membership cards, business cards...

The amulet leapt again. It thudded onto the floor, pinning down an ordinary rectangular card.

"Wow," said Autumn carefully, "that card must have a *lot* of metal in it."

"It must have. Weird." Had he bought that explanation? His expression wasn't giving anything away.

"Are you okay? I mean, is your—? Is everything—?" She realised she was making descriptive hand gestures and stopped.

"It's... all in working order, I think." He bent closer to the ground to look at the card, and Autumn bent with him. "Maitland Picton," he said. There was only an address apart from that: Brightlands on the Close, which was where the poshest of the posh lived, a lane of driveways and lawns and no house numbers, which really annoyed postal workers.

"Who's that?"

"I think she came to talk at the college, a couple of weeks ago. Yeah, that was her. I only met her for a couple of minutes."

"But she gave you her card?"

"I guess she was just handing them out. I could ask

someone if they heard anything else about her."

"Please." She saw that he was smiling, as if he'd been worried that she might never have another reason to call him. But she couldn't deal with that now. "Listen, could I keep this card? I'd like to find out what's in it."

"Me too. Open it up."

"After . . . I do everything else I have to do. You can come back, and I'll show you what's inside. Promise."

They stood, and he seemed annoyed that she'd made him a promise like he was a child. It kind of annoyed her too. "So, I was thinking, we haven't been out on a date in a while . . ."

"Luke, I'm so busy—"

"Okay. Are we still going out?"

"Yes." That had come out without her even thinking about it. "This is just stuff. That's getting in the way. But it won't be this way forever. I'm sorry."

"Okay." He hesitated, as if expecting a kiss, then, when she hesitated too, headed for the door. "Let me know about the magnetism."

She watched him go. Oh, she wanted to. In so many ways. Metaphor had crashed into reality, again. But now, she had work to do. Who the hell was this Maitland Picton?

Judith had written stories in her youth. They'd been very naïve stories, about magical lands and creatures. She'd been extremely influenced by Tolkien. She'd filled volumes. When she'd discovered that there actually were magical lands and creatures, she'd stopped. That moment of discovery, her hair dripping with the waters of the well in the woods, Mother Roseborough laughing, bucket in hand, a few of them standing there, all naked . . . that moment had been a long moment, several months of ecstatic discovery, of marching excitedly through all the new dimensions of forest and lands beyond forest. She'd always thought she'd get back to her stories one day, only they'd now be informed by all she knew. But then, the realities of magic had started to cudgel and betray and lure her. And soon Mother Roseborough was gone, and all Judith's friends and supporters were gone, and she'd made bad alliances, and she was cursed, deep in guilt, never to fully find her way from it, and the old Judith Mawson was born from the young.

She realised she was standing now at the edge of a ploughed field, by a forested track between the new estates and the school. It was night. She was well wrapped up, at least. Some part of her had made her put her coat on. That wasn't always true when she ventured out after Shaun had left her. Which she did often, now she remembered. For some reason. Well, if Shaun really wanted her to stay put, he should lock her in. The rise of the field, the edge of the world with the half-moon above it, a clear cold sky but for some wisps of cloud, was a glorious sight tonight. The soil shone with the life waiting beneath it.

New life. That was a good thought. That felt like summat she could hold on to. Not that she could, in the end, hold on to anything. It were too late for that.

What had she been thinking about? Oh ah. She'd just been remembering in beautiful detail, remembering her stories. There was the upside—all the things she hadn't previously remembered that now she could. It was like a slow rehearsal of everything before the ending. She'd given up fiction for magic, but magic was like stories, so like stories in every way. Magic was about telling, spieling, spelling. Saying something into the world.

Stories have endings.

Oh, she was going to have to be brave. Still, it was easier to be brave when you didn't have a choice. She looked in her bag and found she still had a few posters left. There was some postering that had to be done at night. Who'd told her that? No idea.

She had a strange thought in her head. It was that she'd come out here for some reason of her own. This was one of those places in Lychford where the shape of the land let you feel what influences were working on you. She'd been cursed a few times in her life, in one major way and several minor, and she'd always come here then, having chanced across the place, then worked out what it could do. What was the shape of the land telling her now? That there were two presences influencing her. They were both terrifying. As she let her mind feel them out, she glimpsed the truth of them, just for a second. She couldn't help but cry out. Her mind fled the touch. The sound of her voice in the air scared her all over again. And then her thoughts fled her again, and there was nothing but memories.

And then later, she was leaning on a fence. Where was she? Oh ah. There was that field. Why was she here, again? No idea.

She took one last look at the field and went on her way. Her sister walked beside her. Out of the other side of her vision, Judith saw a new path swinging around across the field, the near end of it following her like the beam of a searchlight. It made her shiver.

Her sister took her arm. "All be over soon," she said.

———————

The next day, in the morning, after she'd opened up the church, Lizzie went over to Witches and knocked on the door.

The Autumn who opened the door was the one Lizzie

had got used to in the last couple of weeks. Every muscle in her face was tense. Her eyes were deep pits, and her hair was even more ridiculously chaotic than usual.

"Something came through the boundaries," she said, without even a greeting. "My detector hit my boyfriend in the balls."

"Wow," said Lizzie, "that sounds like the first two lines of a really weird musical."

"Yeah. Sorry. Come on in."

She led Lizzie inside and locked the door behind her. Lizzie persuaded Autumn to let her make tea before Autumn started explaining. After they'd had three calming sips of whatever this was Autumn kept in the most ordinary looking caddy in her kitchen, Autumn seemed to not be able to take the calm any longer and leapt up to start telling her, with hand gestures, a story about a pendant, a business card, and, indeed, her boyfriend's balls.

"Ouch," said Lizzie. "So are you and he . . . ?"

"Moving swiftly on—"

"No."

Autumn rolled her eyes. "I don't know. Maybe doing this, being the new wise woman, I shouldn't have a boyfriend."

"Judith is *still* the wise woman."

"So, what, I shouldn't be trying to step up? Do you really think we can still leave it to her?"

"I mean you shouldn't let this ruin the other parts of your life. If we asked Judith about this, maybe she'd know—"

"I don't want to put any more stress on her. I might find something to help her. I don't want her to get any worse in the meantime."

Lizzie wanted to say this was too much. But Autumn clearly knew that. She was a grown-up. All Lizzie could really do was be here for her. "Also, Judith didn't do this alone. She had a husband."

"Who turned out to be dead, mostly, so he didn't get in the way."

"You sound like Judith."

Autumn raised her hands in surrender. "Well, maybe I'm turning into her, dementia and all."

Lizzie took that opportunity to share with Autumn what Shaun had told her. "Shaun's doing okay, but I think he's being optimistic about his mum's condition."

"Yeah. We need to be ready for her to go into some kind of . . . home. God, what if she did go into one and started randomly doing spells? It'd be like handing them a bomb."

That thought hadn't actually occurred to Lizzie. It was another awful bump in the road ahead. She put it aside for now. "So, getting back to your worrying news of right this minute, have you found out anything about this Maitland Picton?"

"I have, and it's even more worrying. I was going to ask if you'd heard of her. I thought you knew everyone posh."

Lizzie had to admit that was indeed the demographic of a large part of her congregation. But she had no idea about this one. "I'm trying to think of where that house is on the Close. I'm not sure I know it."

"That might not be a coincidence." Autumn led Lizzie into her workroom, where printouts and files were spread on the big table. On top of them lay a stone on the end of a chain. This, Lizzie assumed, was the pendant that had so painfully intercepted Luke's nethers. Autumn picked it up, started it swinging, and it suddenly stiffened, in an absurd, cartoonlike manner, pointing ramrod straight to . . . Autumn put her finger on the paper. "Mrs. Maitland Picton, on the electoral roll."

"Wow. How does it know there's anything special about her, just from a name on a card or paper?"

"That was the first thing I wondered. But it's not just a name on paper." Autumn went to a drawer and came back with a handful of red dust. She sprinkled it onto the paper. It formed a rough circle around the name and address, as if every particle had been pushed aside and wouldn't fall on those details. "I think this isn't just a record of something, but an . . . alteration to reality, an alteration that's present in the data in the town council office computers, onscreen when that data is displayed, and even when it's printed out, like on the business card Luke had. It's like the magical version of a computer virus, a way to force an idea into the world."

Lizzie realised, with a shiver, that she'd experienced something similar last Christmas, when that couple who turned out not to actually be human beings had changed her perceptions. "So why can't I think of where she lives?"

"I think maybe part of the . . . code . . . is that the special senses you and I have aren't set off by this stuff."

"Almost like it's been programmed to deal with us."

"Yep. But it wasn't prepared to deal with this pendant. So whoever we're dealing with is clever, but we're still one step ahead. I'm going to go have a look at the house this afternoon."

"Are you sure we shouldn't get Judith to—"

"I will if you really want to, if you think it'll do any good."

Lizzie considered. "We should go see her anyway, find out how together she is."

"Okay. Tomorrow. I might have more of an idea what we're dealing with."

"Have you heard from Finn?"

"No. There's nothing coming out of fairy. I think maybe they *are* having some sort of . . . civil war. Maybe Finn's dad has been overthrown. If Finn was okay, and could get a message to me, I know he would have. So . . ." She had to stop talking or, Lizzie sensed, she'd have started to cry. She put a hand to her own brow and closed her eyes.

Lizzie gave her a moment and sipped her tea.

"Don't do that," said Autumn, after a second. "I need to keep going. The world needs me to."

"You need to let me help too."

"I am. You're here. I've also been researching the rest of Maitland Picton's life." She picked up several of the pieces of paper and showed them to her. "Every detail of an everyday—well, posh person—human existence is here. There are records of what school she went to, a Facebook page, land ownership details . . . and all of that makes my detector prick up, but not my senses. I talked to the lady down the third charity shop on the church road, because she's posh, and she couldn't remember anything about Picton, but she was sure she'd been to school with her. It's all a lie."

"That's pretty powerful stuff. So we think she's here in Lychford to . . . ?"

"To, I should think, take a look around and report back to whatever weird shit is waiting out there to invade."

Lizzie felt scared and angry and determined at the same time. Just for once, they were ahead of the game.

"Autumn, this is amazing. I mean, we've actually got the drop on her. We could go over to her house right now—"

"No. Lizzie, we don't know who she is or what she can do. Maybe Judith could just march up and have her, but for me, discovering something exists is one thing, actually leading a confrontation . . ."

Lizzie wasn't sure how much this was lack of confidence talking, and how much was good sense. Perhaps this was the time to err on the side of caution. "So, what do we do?"

"Luke asked around at his college about Maitland Picton. Nobody seems to remember why she was there. She gets around. The records of various local bodies show that she's actually a member of just about all of them."

"Anything directly church related?"

"No."

"Hmm. Indicative."

"Hey. *Most* people in this town aren't—"

"I'm just going to raise an eyebrow and say 'indicative' again."

"But, getting swiftly past that, one of those organisations is meeting tonight. And even if it isn't church related, the local vicar would have some good reasons to pop along."

Lizzie took a big slurp of her tea and restrained the urge to make a sudden little noise of panic.

———————

"Good to see you, Reverend. You're item thirty-eight on the agenda." Lizzie had called ahead to the formidable chair of the Lychford Festival, Carrie Anne Christopher, to make sure she would indeed be welcome at her committee's second to last meeting before the big day, but it turned out that one purpose of that meeting was to make sure of links with other local organisations. Lizzie had told her she'd be doing just that. So she had had to think of some plausible ways her congregation, who were usually agnostic about big local events that could be a bit noisy, might want to get involved. And she'd come up with a few. But now she was sitting at the end of the big committee table in the pavilion of Lychford Cricket Club, she wasn't so sure. Historically, the Festival and the cricket club had always been inseparable, the Festival being held on the cricket club's grounds, and the cricket club running the bar. An entirely separate festival, Lychfest, was held, two weeks ago this year, with the cooperation of the rugby club. If there had been some sort of schism, decades ago, nobody talked of it. One of the non-magical things about Lychford that always surprised Lizzie was the way that civic life was formed of bubbles of committees and bingo nights and charity trusts that hardly interacted with each other, and which each formed almost the entire social life of those involved, to the point where most of those groups assumed their members were the leading civic dignitaries of the town. It was exactly the same as nobody knowing they were on the borders of entire magical realms, the inhabitants of which, thank God, they didn't have to be aware of. And there was another metaphor here, about how a lot of the people in those bubbles weren't aware of the poverty in their own town, of how close to going hungry a lot of the young families in the new estates often were. In their own way, these two festivals, by cooperating with two sports clubs, and by trying to provide something for the whole community, showed a radical—in Lychfordian terms—commitment to outreach.

Of the people in this room, the only ones Lizzie already knew were the two former mayors, who were both also former chairs of the Festival (honours tended to cluster like that, in the spaces where the bubbles met and rubbed along) and Samantha Adkins, who ran the freesheet *The Lychford Answer,* and therefore was the local media. She smiled at those three, the tacticians, the politicians, all twinkly and chuckling and hard as nails.

Carrie Anne Christopher was something in advertising, in a business suit tonight, straight from work, with a look on her face that said she had a lot of plates to juggle, but as long as you were prepared to be spun, everything would be fine. On each side of her were what looked like her good and bad influences, a blond woman with glasses who worked for the town council, and a dark-haired woman with elfin features, who looked like she was about to suggest everyone should bunk off and get some wine. Was either of these Maitland Picton? Lizzie looked around the table. She knew the types from all the different committees she herself was a member of: giggly craftswoman with curly hair, the one who'd make bunting by the mile; serene swan of artiness, the quiet one—something professional, probably in design, going by the outfit; tough old lady, the sort who'd have bolt cutters in her handbag; happy squirrel, definitely the accountant; and the one who was already laughing, the class joker. She probably wasn't Picton. But any of the others could be. Was Lizzie going to get introductions? Could she ask for them? Maybe not with thirty-seven other items on the agenda.

"Let's start with apologies for absence ... none."

"Oh, I have something to add to item six, the fete," said the bunting maker. And then they were off, all interrupting each other, the blond one having to flip between pages to take the minutes as the agenda dissolved into a sort of bureaucratic freeform jazz. In the blur, Lizzie gathered that there had been complaints about the latest round of Festival posters being put in the way of other peoples' posters and in places posters shouldn't be, the responsibility for which wasn't quite nailed down, that one of the bands was suddenly charging more money, and that the matter of who got to sell cakes to those returning from the Saturday morning parade sounded like it required a truth and reconciliation commission. She found she wanted to put her hand up, or, actually, eventually, scream. She'd decided she had to at least say something or have any ability to discover anything here get lost in the chaos, when the door opened.

"Sorry I'm late." The woman was tall, in her late sixties, immaculately dressed, tweed and shawl, silver hair, hardly a line on her face. She looked something like a predatory bird.

"You're just in time for the cookery tent, the art show, and the literary festival," said Carrie.

"All are proceeding to plan. I've sent the mailing list an email with all the details. There's nothing for you to worry about in all three tents. Here's a printout." She slid it across the table.

"What would we do without you, Maitland?" sighed Carrie. "You're just what we need."

And so that was where Lizzie's attention was for the rest of the meeting. So much so that she was startled by item thirty-eight arriving, straight after item seven, and had to blunder her way through a vague promise of support on the day. Maitland watched her, one eyebrow raised, as if she were a preposterous interloper.

Afterwards, with the reminder that there was one more meeting to go, a couple of days before the Festival, the committee members leapt up, all seemingly with busy lives and families to get back to. Maitland was still in a corner, signing cheques for secret squirrel, three other committee members waiting to speak to her. Lizzie found one of the former mayors, Boffy, a smiley older lady with a certain steel behind the eyes. She indicated Maitland. "Why haven't I met her before?"

"You know what Lychford's like. She's something to do with . . . Now which committee was that?" Lizzie could see the enormous databank between Boffy's ears being consulted. "I think she's W.I."

"What are the W.I. like these days?"

"Oh, you know, same as ever. Evil."

Lizzie was sure that whatever evil it was the Women's Institute were rumoured to be a part of, and there always seemed to be something, it wasn't in the same league as what Maitland Picton might represent. But she tended to shy away from the ancient enmities that lurked between local organisations. Across the room, Maitland Picton looked up from her work and made eye contact. Was that a smirk?

"Before I go," she called out, swiftly turning away, "is there anything else anyone wants?"

"You can make me tall," called out the bunting maker.

"I'd like the body of a Kardashian," said the darker-haired of Carrie's two lieutenants. There was general laughter. Having seen this happy lot at work, apart from how they ran the agenda, Lizzie rather wished she had time to be part of yet another committee. She felt angry that Picton seemed somehow to have gotten to the heart of them. Every organisation needed something, she supposed, and someone who could roll in and provide as well as she seemed to be doing would swiftly be embraced.

"I'll have to see what I can do," said Picton. And was it Lizzie's imagination or did Picton's gaze meet her own again, just for a moment?

———————

Lizzie made her way home across the cricket field. The crowd behind her went their separate ways, and she found herself heading alone back toward the far gate to the main road. It was a perfectly clear night above. The autumn cold was indicating that the real darkness was coming. For Lizzie, in the heart of the dark was Christmas. But she also knew, better than everyone she'd just left, better than Carrie Anne Christopher back there, switching the lights off in the pavilion, how deep that darkness could be.

She'd lost Maitland Picton in the crowd. She had seemed to leave very fast. Lizzie had had half a thought of following her. She called Autumn but got her voicemail. She left a message saying she'd seen the enemy, and indeed, there hadn't seemed to be anything about her which triggered Lizzie's special senses. But there was definitely something about her which triggered her community senses.

"You should be the one to visit the W.I.," she was saying, when she saw something ahead. The gap of the gate was lit by the lights of the main road. And at that gap stood a figure.

It was a silhouette. Like the man from a road sign come to life. Like one of the figures Judith had described encountering, at the time when that supermarket chain was seeking to set up in Lychford with supernatural aims and means. Lizzie blinked, and suddenly the silhouette had a proper shape.

Lizzie could have turned and run, headed for the other gate, gone the long way home. But hadn't her whole purpose tonight been to discover the aims of the enemy? Besides, she had a terrible nightmare feeling that if she ran, this thing might run after her, and catch her long before she got to the lights.

Of which the last one now went out.

She heard the distant clang of a gate being locked behind her. She kept walking forward. She said a prayer inside, felt the strength of her God.

"Autumn," she said into her phone, "if I don't come to see you in the next half hour, it's because Maitland Picton's zapped me at the back gate to the cricket field." She clicked off the call, switched on the voice recorder app and pocketed the phone. At least she could leave some evidence for Autumn to find.

She came to the gate. There indeed stood Maitland. She was making no pretence of having a reason to be there. She was calm, stony faced. "Reverend. I thought we should have a word."

Lizzie stepped up to show that she wasn't afraid. A car drove past in the dark, the headlights washing over them. Maitland's eyes flashed like a cat's. Lizzie put her hand on the dry stone of the boundary wall. "What can I do for you, Mrs. . . . ?"

"I believe you know my name."

Suddenly Lizzie didn't want to say it. "Lovely night, isn't it?"

"Oh, should we observe the pleasantries? Very well.

You can almost see my home from here." She pointed upward.

Lizzie almost laughed. She turned her head to look. All she saw were stars. Picton seemed to be pointing at a specific constellation, but it wasn't anything she recognised. "What, are you an alien?"

"Not at all. We've been here longer than you have. But that's one way I could get home from here."

Lizzie realised that Maitland had literally added an extra dimension to the matter of a town surrounded by mystic borders. Which was pretty enormous. How did that square with what Judith had always said about the borders being akin to what you found on everyday maps? Lizzie decided that whatever the truth of this was, she was damn well going to maintain a flippant tone of voice. "Ah, so you're from Neverland? You know, first star on the right—?"

"—and straight on 'til morning. And it's actually 'second star.' I can finish any quote you fancy testing me with. My 'human being' is very good."

Lizzie hoped her expression didn't reveal that she hadn't been testing Picton, she'd just got the quote wrong. "Touché. So any supposed *Mr.* Picton—?"

"People will remember having met him, but we didn't feel he had to be as real as I am."

Lizzie noted the "we." "And how real are you?"

"Well, I'm enjoying being a person here, but it's not what I like to wear when I'm at home. I'm more of a mixture, a recipe."

"A computer virus."

"Goodness, I much prefer my metaphor to yours. Let's just say you're full of meat, and I'm full of ideas."

"So you know who I am, also? I mean, who I hang around with?" Lizzie had really wanted that to sound tougher than it had come out.

"The three of you, yes. The coven."

"We're not a coven. I'm not part of a coven."

"You mean you wouldn't like your bishop to find out you're in a coven."

"Being in a coven would involve me actually having been initiated into a coven."

"Like when you had the water from the well in the woods thrown on you?"

Lizzie stopped. "Nobody *said* that was—anyway, how did you know about that? How do you know our business? What do you want here?"

Maitland suddenly smiled. Lizzie realised that little anxious outburst had put her foe completely at ease. "We've really got off on the wrong foot. Lizzie, may I call you Lizzie?"

"No."

"Lizzie, what do *you* want?"

"In what way?"

"There are all sorts of ways I can help this town. That's what I'm doing here, offering help. I'm not some sort of spy, if that's what you thought. As you say, I clearly know all there is to know about this world already. You see, I come from a place where wishes literally come true."

"You mean you work for Disney?"

"Listen. When I ask you what you want, you can ask for anything, and you'll get it. For instance, you could have your husband back. I mean, I grant you, that's a big ask. I probably couldn't do many other favours that week, but—"

Lizzie found she was suddenly furious. She felt the tears on her face. She'd had no idea that was still so close to the surface. But no, there it was. Fear had brought it all churning up again. "Get behind me," she whispered.

"No, listen, don't go all religious on me. You really can have—"

Lizzie pushed past her, wanting to literally put this thing, whatever it was, behind her. She had already done this, she had already faced supernatural temptation when the boss of that supermarket chain had offered her a huge sum of money, and she had burned that money. She wasn't even intrigued by the offer this time, just insulted. So that was one thing this being hadn't understood about her.

Maitland Picton put a phenomenally strong hand on her shoulder. "You only get one chance," she said.

Lizzie didn't dignify that with a reply. She shoved the hand from her shoulder—which was more about Maitland deliberately letting go—and marched off. She didn't look behind her until she got to the corner. When she did, Maitland was gone. Lizzie fell against the wall and couldn't hold back her tears.

2

JUDITH WAS IN HER ATTIC, looking through her boxes. Moonlight shone through the holes in the felt roofing, so much so that she didn't really need her torch. She had no idea why she was here, but she felt a determination inside her so strong that it scared her and she was just following it. She wished she understood what she was seeing. There were some old boxes here and what was inside . . . the boxes and whatever items they'd contained had decayed together, into a mass of mould and fungi. Bollocks. This wasn't going to be easy, then. But she knew that, for some reason, she had to do this anyway. She broke off a piece of the black decay and put it into her mouth. It reminded her of liquorice, and then she was eating liquorice. Well, that was better! What a good idea of hers this had been! She grabbed handfuls of it, gobbled it up, sliding it back past her lack of teeth, until her mouth was too full, and she had to cough some of it up. Oh, it was like Christmas morning, eating too much. She knelt there, laughing her head off, so happy to see her dad falling back in his chair, his hands over his eyes at how fast she'd gobbled up her treat.

"Your eyes are bigger than your stomach," he said.

It felt like her eyes were pretty wide.

"What are you looking for?" asked her sister.

"T'other thing I came up here for. The books where I wrote my stories.'"

"Why do you want them?"

"Because they'll tell me the truth. In the world, people can tell lies, real lies, lies that dun't work to any pattern, but in stories there's always a shape that makes it obvious who's lying. In stories, you have someone saying a lie, and the people reading will feel cheated unless there's a little clue that it's a lie."

"So you're looking for the truth up here?"

"If you want to put it in a daft way, s'pose I am."

"Well, you're still a long way from it, my dear." Doreen reached out and stroked her hair. "You're a long way from anywhere."

Judith made a face and looked around some more. She pushed over a pile of rotting stuff. Ah. There it were. The box only she could see, because she'd locked up her stories where nothing could get at them. The spells she'd put on this were strong and decades old, from the time when she first knew magic. She'd shielded this box with all she had because here was what she didn't want anyone seeing and mocking, here was what she was always planning on getting back to. Such childish reasons.

She opened the box. And there were her old books. The notebooks in which she'd written her stories. Even the young warlock she'd fallen in love with hadn't seen what was in here.

She took a pen from her pocket and wrote, experimentally, a few sentences. Her handwriting was weak, spidery, all over the place. It took such an effort of will just to move her hand in the right way. Even that had nearly left her now. But now she was close to the box, she knew she had to.

Finally, she was done. She'd made a new story. Such a small thing. Just a gesture. And why? What was it for? Even near the box, she couldn't remember now. She put the book and pen in the pocket of her coat.

Judith took hold of her sister's arm and got to her feet. It was cold up here, she realised. The cold was getting deep into her. And she seemed to have eaten something that disagreed with her. She pointed to the roof. "Is that path still out there?"

"Oh ah. It'll stay put now. No getting away from it."

"So long as I know." Judith nodded, making an effort to keep down the contents of her stomach. "I need a glass of milk now," she said. "And then I'd better see if the two of them need my help yet." Talking to herself, she went back to the trapdoor and, very slowly, descended the ladder.

―――――――

That afternoon, Autumn had indeed gone to inspect Maitland Picton's house, but had found it just as she'd expected: a normal house for normal people, completely unexciting to her senses. She had wandered around uselessly outside it for a bit, but as the only person of colour in the village, hanging around at one of the rich houses . . . She knew the worst that would probably happen in a seemingly sleepy town like this one was stern looks and raised eyebrows, but that probably was still enough to stop her from staying too long.

She'd gone back to her shop, locked the door, and immersed herself once again in her research, ignoring the phone until she'd decided it was time for a break. Then she'd checked her voicemail, nearly dropped her coffee mug, unbolted her door, and rushed out onto the street, only to run straight into Lizzie. Who cried out in shock.

"Oh, thank God!" said Autumn.

"Maybe you could, in the current emergency," panted Lizzie, "answer your bloody phone? And do you have any whiskey?"

―――――――

They sat up with hot toddies. Lizzie told Autumn the whole story, and the more Autumn heard, the more angry she became. Lizzie seemed to have been genuinely scared by Picton. And her knowing about Lizzie's ex-husband, trying to use that as a bargaining tool, made it even worse. "So she tried to get you to ask for something. It sounds like she's doing the 'granting wishes' thing. That's always bad news in stories."

Lizzie nodded. "When she told me she could bring him back to life . . . I mean, doesn't she think we've seen any movies about that shit? Does she come from a world without *Buffy*?"

"I thought you were going to say it was against your religion."

"We are actually about bringing people back to life. Just . . . not like that!"

Autumn realised that Lizzie was still shaking. She put her arms around her. "What's important is you were very brave. If she offered to find me true love forever or something—"

Lizzie immediately perked up. "With Luke?"

"Will you please stop being so interested in that even when you've been shaken up? Right now I'd just like to feel comfortable enough to go on a date with him." She realised magical powers might be listening and called up to the ceiling. "That's not a wish."

"Because if you did wish for that you'd get—"

"Something like only having one date with him ever again, probably, something from the department of ironic punishments. Like in *The Simpsons*."

"Right. But in the stories, it's always the precise legal wording that gets you."

The shop bell rang. Autumn looked to Lizzie. "Stay here." She grabbed from her pocket the protective herbs and charms she now always kept with her and headed into the shop front, only to find Lizzie immediately behind her. "Or don't."

"If she's come after me, I might be able to ward her off with a blessing or something."

Autumn didn't want to argue. She unlocked the door as quickly as she could and flung it open. There stood Judith. "What time is it?" Judith asked, peering up at the sky in surprise. "I think my watch must be wrong."

———

They called Shaun, who said he'd come over at the end of his shift, in about an hour. So they made Judith comfortable in front of the fire. "What's up?" she said, which was an expression Lizzie had never heard her use before.

"Nothing much," lied Autumn, putting a cup of warm—and what Lizzie hoped was ordinary—tea into

Judith's hands. Lizzie was coming down from her own terror, a little ashamed at how much Picton had got to her. It had been the woman's sheer confidence, the way she'd had all the cards ready to play. Her small improvisations had seemed so slight in the face of that. Lizzie looked to Autumn, wondering if, therefore, it was really a good idea not to at least try to involve Judith in all this. Autumn just quickly shook her head. Lizzie sniffed and realised there was a strange smell about Judith. She moved a little closer. Yes, there was something horrible on her breath. God, was she forgetting to brush her teeth now? Her mouth was also discoloured, like she'd been eating . . . oh no, what had been going on here? Lizzie got a wipe from a box on the counter and dabbed at the old woman's mouth until she slapped her hand away.

"Only I were wondering," said Judith, "if there weren't anything I could be helping with? Around the house. I mean the shop. Stupid old woman. I work here! Isn't it time we were opening?"

"Judith," said Autumn, "it's eleven o'clock at night." Lizzie made a mental note to tell Autumn that it wasn't good practice to argue with people with dementia. Distraction was what they should do to make her feel more comfortable. If that was really all they were going to do.

"Oh. Well then, no wonder you don't get any customers."

Autumn laughed. She reached out and smoothed Judith's hair, which made the old woman frown at her. "What's that for? Not like you. My sister Doreen were just doing that. You should pay me more money, all I do around here. So there's nothing I can do?"

"Not tonight."

"Nothing magical's going on, then?"

Lizzie saw Autumn look at her awkwardly. Okay, here it was.

"Yes, there is," Lizzie said, "and we're not sure what we're dealing with. Maybe you can help us." And she described her scary encounter.

"Oh, one of them!" chuckled Judith. She stared off into the distance.

"One of what?" asked Autumn, finally.

"One of what?" asked Judith. "Oh. Right. I last met a cappy in 1975, I think it were. They talk a lot of nonsense, like to puff themselves up, but they're just after attention. What she'll be doing is telling everyone she can sort out everything they need and whizzing around putting all her time into doing all the real world things that need doing to make those things happen, setting them up, when they see she's made stuff come true, for making even bigger wishes."

"Like being taller, or having the body of a Kardashian," Lizzie said, recalling some of the things the Festival committee had wished for.

"Only she don't have the power to do anything about that. The trickster cappy will make people think she can grant everyone's wishes, and she'll soak up the praise, and then, just when they're thinking all their desires, big and small, might actually happen, she'll vanish, with a sort of echoey laughter, and leave them all in the lurch."

"Sort of like an anti . . . genie?" said Lizzie. Was that really all there was to it? She found it hard to imagine that the worst-case scenario for the creature she'd been so scared by was a slightly disappointing local festival.

"Exactly. You look into her, there'll be dozens of people she's promised stuff to, all over town, all being set up for a fall."

"So she won't . . . play tricks on the people asking for things?" asked Autumn, sounding almost disappointed.

"No. She dun't have the power." She looked to Lizzie. "Dun't have the power to bring your lad back either. Sorry to say."

"I'm not disappointed," she said. She wouldn't give this thing that. She'd never heard of this creature, not in all the time Judith had mumbled away to them about arcane lore. That was weird, wasn't it? Well, she supposed Judith was the wise woman in the room, and her subject matter was pretty enormous. She could never have told them everything. "Where's this thing from?"

"Dunno," said Judith. "I never followed one and went

to see. Why, did she say she was from somewhere?"

Lizzie went to stand in the middle of the room, thought for a moment, and, remembering exactly the pose Maitland Picton had struck, pointed upward. Judith wandered over and looked up along her raised arm. "Well, that dun't tell me anything, you'd need to be in the same place she were, at the same time of night, then I could tell you the stars."

Autumn sighed. "Is there anything else you can tell us about this . . . cappy?"

"Small fry. It likes the sound of people clapping, and it dun't like the sound of disbelief and mockery. Confidence player, if you like. If you want to drive it off, just boo it a bit and it'll get all ruffled and march off home. Like a lot of people. But it's probably not worth the bother. Leave well alone if I were you. What's the worst that could happen?" She stared off into space for a moment, then seemed to snap back to reality. "Oh. While you're here, Reverend, there's something serious we have to talk about."

"What is it?" Lizzie wanted to put her hand on Judith, but got the feeling that, in this moment of being very serious, the old woman wouldn't have welcomed it.

"I want you to take the funeral."

"You mean . . . your funeral?"

"Well, whose do you think I mean?"

Autumn looked a little annoyed. "Judith, wouldn't you prefer something pagan? I've got some ceremonies we could look at—"

Judith suddenly yelled. "Whose funeral is it? The wise woman and the vicar are friends. That's how it's always been. She's the vicar. She's . . . a friend." That had tripped up her tirade. The emotion of that Lizzie had found hard to bear. Judith took a long breath through her nose and composed herself. "That's it."

"I'm sorry," said Autumn.

Judith just closed her eyes and shook her head. "You'll miss me when I'm gone. I'll miss you. Journey we're all on. How you two are going to keep warm I don't know."

Lizzie went to Autumn and took her arm. Autumn was shaking, trying not to show how much she was feeling.

"Goodbye," said Judith. "Off on the road. And I won't see you both. Or I will. One of you. At the end, have to."

A car slowed to a halt outside the shop. That, thought Lizzie, would be Shaun. She wondered if he'd seen Judith as far gone as this.

Autumn gently disengaged from Lizzie and went to the old woman again. "Judith, before you go, I just want to make sure. About the help you've just given us." Judith's eyes were suddenly alert again, and Lizzie felt she agreed with Autumn's decision to ask about this a second time. Getting back to her business seemed to give back

Judith some of her dignity. "You're sure that, for this creature, this cappy, it's not about granting wishes in ironic
and awful ways?"

"No," said Judith. "Why would it be?"

"Because that's how it always is with wishes in stories."

The bell rang. Judith got slowly to her feet and went
to it. They went with her. She stopped on the threshold.
"Magic," she said, "isn't like stories." There was such pain
in her voice that it took an effort for Lizzie herself not to
start crying.

———————

Next Tuesday evening, Autumn went to the town hall for
the monthly meeting of the W.I. After Judith's late-night
visit to the shop, Autumn and Lizzie had taken turns visiting the old woman at home every day, but those visits
had been hard work. Judith now didn't seem to remember anything about that visit, or about "cappies." And
Autumn couldn't find anything about any such creature
online, or in any of her books. How was this even meant
to work? Surely the people Maitland had promised the
biggest things to, the impossible things, wouldn't actually
be expecting them to happen, so where was the fun for
her in that? Still, Autumn knew how secret knowledge
was kept in weird corners. She couldn't shake the feeling

that something that offered to grant wishes really should be capable of doing so, and that those wishes should come with horrible reversals. Magic, to Autumn, had always felt like a story being told, whatever Judith had said. She'd been on her way to thinking it was a narrative version of science, in that it connected things poetically. And yet, here was Judith saying that wasn't true. Perhaps what was going on here was that Autumn's view was that of a novice, and Judith could see the larger picture. Or was that just imposter syndrome talking? At any rate, in the end, Autumn and Lizzie between them had decided to make sure of the details of what Judith had revealed to them. Hence this visit.

The hall car park was full, and there were old ladies and, reassuringly, several younger ones, in big coats, smelling magnificent, milling about and talking to each other. There were friendly greetings as she headed in. The Women's Institute was a worldwide organisation that still, to Autumn, had a feeling of frumpishness about it. All "Jam and 'Jerusalem,'" as Lizzie had once put it. Their reputation for "evil," which Lizzie had also mentioned, seemed to be because they had, at some point, got in the face of virtually every other organisation in town. They seemed to stick up for themselves. Which Autumn couldn't bring herself to think was a bad thing.

She found the hall bustling, with chairs laid out for an

audience, and a desk in front of the stage, where women were gathering, talking, and handing out leaflets. There was that civic polish smell that included old wood and tea bags left too long, which always made Autumn feel both comforted and slightly wary. She found a chair near the back. Swiftly, the spaces around her filled up. Soon it was standing room only. A middle-aged white woman in a trouser suit and silk scarf stood by the table and called the meeting to order.

"After the successful motion from Ms. Spencer-Pilkington last week," she began, "you will be happy to hear that we are forgoing the singing of 'Jerusalem.'"

Autumn was surprised by the cheer that erupted around her.

"Rubbish!" shouted a dissenting voice from the back. "It's a socialist marching song!"

"The motion noted," continued the chairwoman, "that the hymn had many meanings, positive as well as negative, but all in all the feeling of the meeting was that the colonialist associations that went with it were oppressive to our sisters in the various African branches of our organisation, a point we shall be putting forcefully to the national council at the next assembly." A cheer rose around her again, punctured only by a single angry noise a second later from the back row. "Now, for Mrs. Caversham-Thoroughgood's report on her visit to the Cheltenham Whole Earth Musical Collective and Jumble Sale."

Autumn couldn't help it. She actually put her fingers to her arm and gently pinched herself.

"They were," she told Lizzie, later that night, "sort of . . . brilliant. And yet also really annoying."

"Evil annoying?" Lizzie was looking at her over the rim of a mug that said *Trust Me, I'm a Vicar*. Lizzie made the strongest coffee Autumn had ever tasted.

"No, really, really good annoying. On my side annoying. Because every now and then I do roll my eyes at how my side does stuff, but then I look at the other side. This lot were so woke. None of them actually congratulated me on my ethnicity, but I was expecting it any minute."

"Wow. I must go along."

"You really should. Because it will be annoying. But also great."

"So why does everyone think they're evil?"

"Because they fight the good fight."

"That's one of my lot's sayings, actually."

"Well, this lot are your lot. They're a Christian organisation. Except they're out there doing good things."

"Hey!"

"I know . . . I mean . . . but *this* lot . . ."

Lizzie sighed at her. "There is no second sentence that is going to make that first one better. But moving swiftly on—no, really, talking over you now—did they say anything about Maitland Picton?"

"Yeah. They got all huffy when I mentioned her name. She made them a lot of what they called 'silly promises,' and then didn't follow through. One of them called her a 'con woman.' They seem to have chucked her out."

"This sounds like Judith described, then. Except—"

"What?"

"She must have upped her game for the Festival committee. I mean, those guys seemed really practical. They wouldn't have stood for her bullshit any more than the W.I. would. To get them onside, she must have followed through with actual hard work."

"Yeah. Maybe she started too loudly at the W.I., realised that, and so came at the Festival with little stuff, stuff she could actually do, and worked her way up?"

"Sounds reasonable."

But Autumn wasn't sure she was convinced by her own theory. What was this, still nagging away at her? "We're missing something. I don't know what."

"We do know, however, that this is a magical creature who's not powerful enough to avoid being kicked out of the W.I."

"Do you reckon we should do something about her, then? I mean, Judith said we're probably able to, and if the W.I. managed it . . ."

"Judith also said we shouldn't bother."

"Yeah." Autumn put her own mug down on the table. This was one of those moments, the big calls she supposed the wise woman had to make. "Still," she said, "I don't like that she had a go at you. And I don't want to let her think she can swan about Lychford, hurting people . . . slightly. Emotionally. Probably. Anyway, I say let's do our job and kick this thing's bottom."

Finding the cappy's bottom in order to kick it proved to be a thing. Lizzie spent every evening that week going between the various town organisations and the various pubs, asking about Maitland Picton. She got fed up with the number of times people told her about consulting various social media as if she were innocent of the ways of the modern world. She and Autumn had decided they didn't want to wait for the next Festival meeting, so they needed another place Picton was likely to be.

They found it at, of all places, the Bowls Club. This was one of a number of local sporting clubs where the majority of the membership didn't actually play the sport. It was more, Lizzie had always thought, a club for people who found bending down to be a feat of competitive athletics. Her conversations there came up with several positive mentions of Picton, that she was in every Monday night for a small glass of sweet sherry. She seemed, according to the members Lizzie talked to, to be a very helpful person, having offered many of them small favours. Yes, she'd followed through with the promised help, be it a recommendation for a window cleaner or showing up to help move some logs. Yes, the work in every case was done in record time, now Lizzie mentioned it.

So, here was an organisation Picton had not yet pissed off, an organisation she was still saying all the right things to and walking the walk as well. Which spoke to her being not so powerful, because what sort of supernatural monster moves logs? So Lizzie signed herself and Autumn up for social membership. On the night, Lizzie told Autumn to wear something relatively smart, so of course Autumn came along in something that would have attracted comment in the cantina from *Star Wars*.

"It was the only dress that wasn't in the wash," said Autumn, sitting down with Lizzie at a small table in the Bowls Club lounge, two halves of 6B in front of them. Neither of them had felt able to give up their drink of choice since they were students for the lure of a small glass of sweet sherry. "While I've been wondering how to protect the world, laundry's been piling up."

Lizzie, as always, was in her black shirt and clerical collar. Autumn, she reflected, always seemed, by association, to make her feel like she was on her way to a costume party.

They made small talk, Lizzie keeping her eye on the door. It wasn't long before Maitland Picton entered, that supercilious look on her face once more. She was greeted with smiles and hugs, but, satisfyingly, when she saw Lizzie and Autumn, her face fell.

"Maitland, over here!" called Lizzie, taking more pleasure in this than she should have allowed herself.

The woman, or being, came over. "I . . . didn't expect to see you here. This must be Autumn."

"Yeah," said Autumn, "it must be, because something's going to fall." And she actually landed that, which Lizzie didn't think she herself could have managed. "Boo."

"What?"

Autumn stood up and pointed at her. "Boo!" She said it long and low, changing it this time from a noise of surprise into a noise of criticism, and as she did so, she slipped onto the table a beer mat that Lizzie had earlier watched her impregnate with a powder she'd burned in a frying pan, which had included cayenne pepper, white pepper, dill, and—less Cordon Bleu and more worryingly—sulphur. At the same time, with her right hand, Autumn began swiftly tracing a diagram in the air which, she had told Lizzie, should trick the people nearby into seeing the reverse of what was actually going on. This had seemed, to Lizzie, to be beyond anything Autumn had tried before, but the apprentice had assured her that she'd been practicing hard. Besides, how welcome at the Bowls Club did they want to be? Which had turned out to be a rhetorical question, because by the time Lizzie had started to say that "really pretty welcome" was her preferred answer, Autumn had already been reaching for her coat.

Lizzie looked to the other patrons, who were smiling at them. Presumably, they were hearing "boo" as applause, or something similar. Now it was time to play her part. Objects and gestures were just for focus. So she didn't use them. She breathed to put herself in the correct mental attitude for prayer and asked for courage and protection. She had been told by her Lord that she would fear no evil, and Maitland Picton was not the shadow of death. Looking at her now, she felt her God and believed in her own courage and felt sorry for Picton. Which was better than feeling pleased at this being's discomfort. Indeed, Lizzie now felt she couldn't join in either the booing or the series of carefully structured insults that Autumn had started to call out, pointing at Picton with each one. "Unwanted. Useless. Meaningless. Leave good folk alone, trickster. You are discovered. You are nothing."

"In a moment, you should find you have to leave," said Lizzie, startling Autumn out of her prepared routine. "Why not talk to us instead, come to some understanding? If you need something, maybe we could help you get it. We don't have to play games."

Autumn looked frustrated at her for a moment, and then nodded. Lizzie knew that Autumn had come to find the notion of borders around the town that just kept everything out, without negotiation or compromise, deeply awful. If her friend had room for mercy now, Lizzie was sure she'd use it.

"Understanding?" barked Picton. "I am what I am! Either do it or don't, but don't toy with me! I'm only here to play my games. I'm a cappy, it's what I do! I'm not hurting anyone! I wouldn't!"

Lizzie hated the pleading tone in the being's voice. And that little speech had been a bundle of mixed messages. At least they knew now that Judith had been correct about the nature of this creature. And that they genuinely didn't have much to fear. "If you can only see one way to play the game," she said, "we'll play our part and send you home. We won't hurt you in doing it."

"Then get on with it!"

Lizzie looked to Autumn and nodded. Mercy enough had been offered.

Autumn finished up her list of curses and lowered her

finger like she was striking the air with a sword. "Done and can't return!"

With a cry of frustration, Maitland Picton blurred into a shape which was suddenly out of the door and gone. The door slammed behind her. The other patrons clapped as if delightful pleasantries had been exchanged. "Phew," said Lizzie. "I can't believe I was that scared of her."

"And we can even come back to the Bowls Club." Autumn looked to the beer mat, which was on fire, and quickly dropped it into her pint. She took a quick breath in, which snuffed out the last of it. Then they both let out a long breath. Autumn's smelt slightly of sulphur. "I can't believe," she said, "that it was so easy."

Lizzie couldn't quite believe that either.

———————

Autumn found that she also was very wary of believing they'd actually done it. Any sense of pride she ever felt these days, following what had happened with her collapsing the borders, was always now tempered by the thought that it would soon be followed by a fall. So they did a bit of checking. An entirely different house now stood where Maitland Picton's had been. The electoral roll now didn't show her name. Everything checked out.

So when, a couple of days later, Autumn knocked on Judith's door, she was looking forward not just to checking in on her, but also to sharing with her that she had done the job of a wise woman and done it well. She couldn't manage "smug" these days, but she hoped Judith might find the news reassuring.

Judith, in her pinny and rubber gloves, opened the door and stared at her. "Yes?"

"Hi, Judith. It's me. Can I come in?"

"If you're collecting for charity, sod off, I don't have any money."

Autumn felt her heart sink a little. She realised that from inside the house she could hear the sound of running water. "Have you left the tap on?"

Judith looked awkward. "What were we going on about?"

Autumn took a risk and gently stepped past her. Judith didn't try to prevent her. Autumn stepped into a kitchen where the floor was covered in water. It was already soaking her shoes. She ran to the sink, where a vast pile of dishes stood in a plastic bowl, and turned off the taps. She turned to look at Judith, who, suddenly, horribly, looked on the verge of tears. "Oh, Judith . . ."

"What have I done?" She said it like the world was coming to an end. "Listen, it's good that you're here, I've summat to show you. You and the reverend. Urgently."

"But what about—?" Autumn gestured to the water.

Judith blinked, as if seeing it for the first time. "Brain of mush," she said. "I'll clean it up. After." And she marched off into the other room.

Autumn quickly followed. Judith's lounge, thankfully, in the way of these old places, was on a slight rise from the kitchen. She pulled out her phone and texted Shaun, asking him to come over, as Judith went over to an old . . . well, some sort of enormous combined radio and record player . . . and picked up a pile of papers and brochures on top of it. "Here you go," she said, and dropped the pile triumphantly onto the coffee table.

Autumn looked at the top page of the file. "Ashdown House Retirement Home."

"It's where Shaun is planning on putting me away."

"Judith, it's not like that—"

"I don't mind him getting ready for that. Except I can still run my own home. But read the bloody thing."

Autumn flipped some pages. And was startled to find them stinging her occult senses. There was a bland promotional picture of a sunny hallway inside the retirement home . . . and it was yelling at her that here was some hidden supernatural evil. "Oh my God."

Judith slumped in her chair and put a hand to her face. "You believe me."

"Yes, I do." On every second page of the prospectus

there was something that screamed out at Autumn. "When did you notice this?"

"Shaun brought that over yesterday. He's wanting me to go for a visit. I'm thinking we all should."

"Absolutely. Do you think this is some sort of . . . trap? I mean, has this all been set up because something's re-alised Shaun's considering this? Or has this always been there?" She couldn't remember feeling anything on the many occasions she'd walked past the place.

"Don't know either way. But we need to do summat."

"Is it all right . . . if Lizzie and I did something, and then reported back to you?"

Judith took a breath, and an angry look flared on her face. But then it went again. "Probably for the best. Especially if it's a trap for me. But in the meantime, there's summat else you can do. Could you stop Shaun from thinking about putting me there? Because I'm going to forget about this, don't argue, you know I am. I might let him."

Autumn felt for the sudden helplessness in Judith's voice. She put her hand on hers. "Don't worry. We'll make sure that doesn't happen."

———

Lizzie couldn't believe the news that Autumn had hammered on her door to tell her. She also couldn't believe that Autumn never remembered that the Vicarage had a perfectly functional doorbell. "Ashdown House? I'm there every other day!"

Autumn plonked a brochure into her hands. It buzzed so hard with dark magic that Lizzie nearly yelled and threw it back. She gingerly turned over the pages. Familiar places were pictured that now reeked of badness. Even staff she knew seemed to be cackling and hissing like fiends.

"Do you want to get your stuff for an exorcism?" said Autumn.

"I don't do those. I have a number I can call for the diocesan delivery minister. Unsurprisingly, given he doesn't know what's really going on in this town, I've never called it. But yeah, let's get over there, right now."

———

They walked through the alley past the nursery, and under the arch that led into the marketplace. Ashdown House was up Sheep Street, past the chip shop. Lizzie didn't need to ring the bell, she just waved through the glass to the receptionist. She looked to Autumn and saw that there was nothing about this place that was setting off her extra senses either. Which was very weird, given what they'd seen in the brochure. She shook her head. "You really have someone you can call?"

"I've been waiting all this time," said Lizzie, as the receptionist buzzed them in, "for you to use that line from *Ghostbusters*. But now you never will."

They explored the place, on the easy pretext of Lizzie visiting some of the residents, and bringing her friend with her to talk about, err, close-up magic. Which Autumn, when Lizzie pressed her, decided to indeed *talk about* rather than demonstrate. "I don't know the stage show version and I'm not risking doing any minor workings when we might be standing in the magical equivalent of an explosives factory," Autumn whispered, after they'd had a lovely chat to a third thankfully rather wandery old person.

"It was all I could think of for you to be here to do a lesson on. I mean, what's more plausible, that or fashion advice?"

"Ouch."

"But do you seriously get the vibe from any part of this building that there's any kind of powder keg going on here?" They walked past a fresco made by local schoolchildren that, in the paperwork, had definitely come over as an *evil* fresco. But now Lizzie couldn't feel any emanation from it other than cuteness. Autumn looked around to make sure nobody was watching and put her palm to it. From the look on her face, she didn't sense anything. She popped out her cheeks and made a tense little noise.

"What are you doing?" asked Lizzie.

"Buttock clench, pulse of inquiry through my lower spine, into my hand, sort of like radar. Poking it really hard." She stepped back from the wall, clearly puzzled. "It was just like talking to, well, a brick wall."

They said their goodbyes, headed out again, and went to the coffee shop that sold the world-famous brownies. There was a garden out the back where, at three o'clock in the afternoon at least, with their coats on against the cold, they could talk in secret. "What *is* this?" said Lizzie.

"It's definitely something," agreed Autumn. "We've had a minor being who tried very hard to have their weirdness only sensed in the paperwork, and now a . . . I don't know, a haunting? Which, again, can only be sensed in the paperwork."

"I'm going to make sure that Shaun doesn't sign Judith up for that place, anyway. I don't have to lie about finding out something real world awful about it, I think he'd take our magical word for it. Plus, he's still not ready to go for it, even after the flood incident."

Autumn had been nodding along, her thoughts clearly

elsewhere. "The cappy thing turned out to be true, so might this. Maybe our senses are somehow on the blink?"

"Oh no," said Lizzie.

"Yeah," sighed Autumn. "I think it's time we re-upped our dose."

The walk to the well in the woods wasn't something either of them were used to doing without Judith. Autumn felt strange to be the one leading the way along that path, which slowly became of impossible length and went in directions only the magical or unlucky would tread. Still, the season after which she was named was making the surroundings beautiful, with every tree this afternoon showing its gown of brown and gold. And yet being out in nature, actually having time to think, made Autumn aware of how little money she was making from the shop at the moment, how being free to see all this during the afternoon made her feel not liberated, but unemployed. The battle against evil was soon going to require her taking out an overdraft.

The signpost that pointed out the footpaths to nearby villages, and to other routes, those that could only be navigated by those that knew, was a familiar feature of this walk, but this time there was something different about it. This time, wrapped around it was . . .

"A poster for the Festival," said Lizzie, inspecting it. "Wow. To even get out here someone must have got very lost. But they brought Sellotape."

"It's kind of worrying," said Autumn. "Maitland Picton on the Festival committee, Festival poster out here . . ." She put a hand to the poster. "But it's not like it's made it an evil signpost. I can still only sense the promise of the directions. Still, better safe than sorry.'" She took a small pair of scissors from her bag, cut the poster from the sign, and put it in her bag. "The Festival wouldn't get much in the way of take-up out here anyway."

They continued on their way and made it to the well in the woods without further incident. Nothing there seemed amiss. The well stood in its isolated glade as it always had, in impossible lands on the borders of so much that went beyond impossible. The leaves had covered the wooden lid over the well itself. Autumn grabbed the lid and hauled it off, freeing the rope that led down to the bucket. "Ready?"

Lizzie shook her head. She put on the ground her shopping bag containing two enormous fluffy towels. "I'll wait until the water's here. I'm not going to strip off before I have to."

"Your catchphrase."

Lizzie stuck her tongue out at her. Autumn grabbed the handle that turned to pull up the bucket and heaved at it. It didn't budge. She remembered Judith doing this without exertion. Wow. Were old lady muscles really that powerful? Lizzie saw what the problem was and came over to help. Together, they tried the wheel again, but it wasn't budging. "Is it stuck?"

Autumn looked down into the well. She could just see the bucket hanging freely at the end of the rope. But what else could she see down there? At the same level as the bucket, there was something stuck to the walls of the well. Four things. Were those . . . ?

"Lizzie," she said, "there are Festival posters down there."

Lizzie looked down there and said something very unclerical. They both grabbed the rope itself and heaved on it, but it resisted them. The bucket didn't budge. It was held there by what must be supernatural forces. Which were somehow connected to the posters. And yet Autumn couldn't feel anything out of the ordinary.

Looking amazed, Lizzie took a step back, and took up a posture which Autumn had come to know. "No," Autumn said quickly, "don't bless the well."

"Why not?"

"Well, it's sort of . . . the basic source of magic around here. What if you kind of . . . get rid of it?"

"I don't think my belief system erases yours."

"Historically—"

"Please don't use the H word, you know what I mean."

"Okay, try it."

Lizzie did. But it made no difference.

Autumn tried a couple of easing and unlocking charms, but nothing was working, the bucket didn't budge. "These posters," she concluded, stepping back from the well and wiping her brow, "are enemy action."

———————

Lizzie watched as Autumn smoothed the poster back out again onto her workbench. "I don't think this is anything to do with the Festival people themselves," Lizzie said.

"No," said Autumn, "I'm thinking this is something Maitland Picton did before we got rid of her. Something she left behind." She showered it with various powders, wiped them away with no visible results. "We're going to have to assume we won't be able to feel the effects. So, when it comes to this stuff we need to rely on our tools."

"Would you object to some holy water?"

"Just because I didn't want you erasing a well doesn't mean that . . . wow, we get to say some odd sentences."

So Lizzie got a cup of water from the tap, blessed it, and, urged by Autumn not to use too much, dotted it onto the poster. Nothing. "Without our extra senses, could we even tell if these tools are working?"

"Yeah, because I can still sense the way my powder of graphite is working, all shifting around in its jar, influenced by the occult weather. So I think I'd know if it was shifting because of this stuff we can't feel."

"And of course, as always, in those terms, I take my holy water on trust." Lizzie used some kitchen paper to wipe it away. "Okay, new approach, maybe it's the words. What does this thing *say*?" Lizzie read the whole poster out loud. It was all pretty much innocuous, talking about the bands and stalls and sporting events. "Look at this, though," she said, indicating a line of smaller print beside a Facebook logo. "'What do you wish the Festival could do for Lychford?' That's a weird way to put it. The use of 'wish'—"

"Lizzie, you're brilliant." Autumn got out her phone and looked up the Festival's Facebook event page. It didn't shine with occult power, but by now neither of them were expecting it to. "I wonder if one of the jobs Picton did for the Festival was tech support?" She found the question from the poster as a separate post from the organisers. "And there are over one hundred comments."

"Oh no. We've had to do some extreme things to save the world—"

"Yeah, we're going to have to read the comments."

So they did. The sheer number of them had struck Lizzie as odd, but now that she read them, she could see why there were so many. The very first comment, by one Meadow Hill, whose profile photo was of three pugs, was a sarcastic comment to the effect that she wished the Festival could make the local youths actually use the skate ramp in the park rather than lounge around it. There then followed many, many more to that effect.

"Just about all of them are making wishes," she said, "implicitly."

"And I can see how a lot of them could come true in ironic ways," said Autumn, puzzled, "but Judith said that wasn't what the cappy was up to. Even if it was, a lot of this is trivial stuff."

"So is it like Judith said, are these just a bunch of wishes that Picton wanted to hear, so she could preen about making some of them come true? Are we just dealing with some . . . magical architecture she left behind? What's all this got to do with the retirement home and us not being able to sense everything?"

"Tonight," said Autumn, decisively, "we take action."

Autumn found herself, as they approached the Plough

that evening, taking pains to explain to Lizzie how "taking action" turned out to mean going down to the pub because this was the local for some of the Festival committee. So, of course, they were doing this tactically.

"Of course," agreed Lizzie.

They'd gone over to Judith's first, but found the lights not on and nobody answering the door. Which, Autumn had said, regretting the words almost as soon as they left her mouth, was a pretty apt metaphor. Lizzie had called Shaun, and they'd been relieved to hear that, when he'd visited, she'd mentioned being tired and going to bed early.

The Plough was the most local of locals in Lychford, and it had taken some courage on Autumn's part to come back here, after the drunken night that had resulted in so much bad news for herself and the town and, well, reality in general. But the worst of that had happened at a different pub. There was a new barman, Robbie, understudy to Rob the landlord, and he seemed to be attracting a younger crowd. "Attracting is the word," said Autumn to Lizzie, as she sat down at their usual table, bringing two pints of 6B.

"Sorry?"

"I saw you making small talk."

"He's got a girlfriend, hasn't he? And I'm still in mourning."

"It's been over a year."

"Has it? I should have put a note in my diary. 'Start dating again from this point.' Also, probably not a good look for the local vicar to be chatting up the bar staff."

"So who are you allowed to chat up?"

"This is a problem those in my profession have faced pretty often, you know."

"And what's the solution?"

Lizzie just smiled angrily at her for a long moment, then thankfully spotted something in the other corner. "Hey, spotlight off me, there's *your* source of awkwardness." Autumn looked over to see Luke sitting alone with his pint, staring into the first fire Rob had lit that year. "Is he still nursing a bruised—?"

"I'd better go check." Autumn evidently saw Lizzie's grin and swatted her around the shoulder. "I mean on how he's doing. You come with."

"Why?"

"I kind of . . . don't know how things are. Lizzie, please—"

Which got Lizzie out of her seat before Autumn could finish the sentence. They went to join Luke, who looked up at them in surprise. "Oh, hi," he said. "I was just going to text you—"

"Sorry," began Autumn, "I should have dropped you a line—"

"—because I just saw that old lady who works at your shop."

Lizzie realised that their mission here tonight wasn't going to work out. "You saw Judith? Where?"

"She was hanging around at the gate by the cricket club. I wondered if she was okay, so I stopped, and she said she was. She got angry with me, told me to get on my way. I thought I should tell somebody who knew her."

Autumn sighed. "Thanks. We'd better get over there and see to her."

Lizzie looked between her and Luke as she headed for the door. "If we manage to get back, I think Autumn would very much like to sit and talk to you, because she was saying she hadn't for ages and was missing you—"

"Lizzie," bellowed Autumn from the doorway, "come on!"

———————

"I can't believe you did that," Autumn could feel the blush on her face as they marched toward the cricket club.

"Sometimes you have to be on the nose about this stuff."

"You were more on the nose than a . . . moustache!"

"I love it when you try for metaphors."

Autumn wanted to say that was kind of a job for her, but they'd reached the road that led past the cricket club. By the gate, under the street light, there indeed stood, stock still, a shape that looked very like Judith. "Oh my God, what's she doing?"

They reached her, only to find her staring into space. Staring into space upward, that was. "Were it around this time?" she said, not even looking around at them or saying hello.

"Judith," said Autumn, feeling so lost to see her here, "we have to get you back home."

"No, wait a second," said Lizzie. Autumn saw she'd matched eyelines with Judith and was now looking up in the same direction she was. At the stars in the clear sky. "Judith, do you mean is it around this time when I encountered Maitland Picton?"

"Well of course I do!" Autumn was cheered to hear that tone in her voice. And now she got what the old witch was saying. She squatted down to look in the right direction too. "You stand where she stood," said Judith. "Now, where did she point?"

Lizzie hesitantly adopted a pointing pose. Autumn could see that she was indicating what might be a constellation, three bright stars and a lesser one, that would form a triangle or a strangely geometrical part of a horse or something. "Because since this is the same time of night, those will be the same stars, won't they?" said Lizzie, who'd obviously seen a few more Brian Cox documentaries. "Where Maitland Picton said she came from."

"Right," said Judith. She looked to Autumn. "You point too. This is going to need both of you."

Autumn got cheek to cheek with Lizzie and raised her arm, then rather awkwardly pointed. It was so good to be working under Judith's guidance again, annoying as she'd always found it in the past. The old hedge witch seemed to have found her mojo again. "So, what are we doing?"

"Being reeled in and landed," said a familiar voice from behind them.

The blood in Autumn's face ran cold. She tried to turn, but realised, with a rush of horror, that she couldn't. She tried to look to Lizzie, beside her, but couldn't even move her eyes. She could only make out the shape of her, as immobile as Autumn was, in her peripheral vision. This posture was already making her muscles ache. She made herself stay calm as a figure walked around them, then nimbly hopped up onto the stone of the gateway, so they could see her. It was Maitland Picton. Autumn wanted to yell something at her, but though she was still breathing, though she could move her chest slightly, she couldn't move whatever she'd used in her throat and lips to form words.

"I'm sure you're discovering the exact bounds of your

confinement," said Picton. "I laid this pattern at this site immediately after my encounter with the reverend. I thought you'd come back here straight away and that at least one of you would point in the direction I pointed, toward stars I have actually nothing to do with. But in the end, it took quite a large nudge to get you here. I had to lure that young man into walking a quite unusual path from his college to that pub so he'd see Judith. Didn't you realise that?"

Her words were having the impact she wanted them to, but for Autumn it was the thought of how Judith was involved in this that was the worst thing. What had this bitch done to her, to make her betray them? She managed a kind of angry noise in the back of her throat.

"You like using the terms of modern technology to describe something totally unlike it. Having said that, you understand how much magic is about story, about 'spooky action at a distance.' So perhaps I could use one of your metaphors back at you. Your Judith has been hacked."

Autumn's mind was racing even as the cold and the ache was settling into her body. Had it been Picton that had caused Judith's dementia? No, that had been the case long before. If only Autumn's own actions hadn't caused Judith to use up so much of her energy, maybe she could have fought off whatever Picton had done to her.

"Judith set you up to adopt that position, which triggered my trap. Judith has been putting up the posters I designed for the Festival committee. Judith lulled you into thinking I was harmless," said Picton, "that I was something called a cappy, a name she made up from her own imagination. Harmlessness and weakness was the impression I'd taken care to leave with the only organisation I'd made a scandal at, the W.I. I made that scandal to make sure you'd hear about it. When you came after me at the Bowls Club, I completed the impression and was able to hide once more, giving me time to finish off my plan. The nature of which I will not tell you. Every move I have made, I have made in order to use your own strengths and expectations against you. Even the accent and style I have adopted I chose to ease my acceptance into this town, and to make you take delight in 'defeating' me. That delight stopped you from checking too carefully for my continuing presence. My masters created me to be undetectable to your senses. But your current situation is because of, I feel, not just ignorance on your part, but a certain arrogance. It seems you've never before encountered a professional. The reverend asked me if I was some sort of spy. I'm not. I'm the *invasion*. I'm the bait your reality has swallowed, just as the lands of fairy are being hooked by one of my colleagues. And soon both territories will be annexed by my people, and considerably improved. Human notions of what is expected of reality and what is not will be turned completely inside out."

Autumn wanted to say something to Picton to encourage her to keep talking, because every detail of this was vital.

But now Picton seemed to be tiring of it. She stretched and yawned. "I'll allow myself a small celebration. But note that it's only after the job is finished. A feature of what you're probably thinking of as my 'stealth magic' here is that you're not only held in place but can't be perceived by other human beings. So nobody's going to rescue you. Your situation will gradually become what I believe was regarded as the worst possible form of medieval torture, the 'little ease,' a cell which is so small that there's no support and one's muscles can't relax. It's the same sort of thing with those people hanging from manacles in cartoons. I should think your muscles are working overtime already. Waste products will build up inside them. This will keep on going, well, until you die from either exposure or lack of water. I'd show mercy by taking off your coats to hasten the process, but I really don't feel like it, considering how your kind have treated every single one of my kind who's ever previously ventured here. I wanted you to know that. You brought this on yourselves."

She hopped down from her perch and went behind them both once again. She muttered a few words to Judith that Autumn couldn't make out. Then she heard them both retreating, at the old witch's pace. Autumn felt her arms and legs starting to hurt from the posture already and tried not to panic.

———————

Judith realised she was walking by the cricket club. She was remembering sunlight on that gorgeously green, flat surface. But now it was night. Now it was winter. She shivered and looked around. Well, there was her sister, Doreen, so that was all right. But who were this posh woman who was also walking with her?

"Have we met?" she asked, putting on airs and graces a bit as, annoying herself, she automatically did when meeting anyone who owned a nice coat.

"You asked for my help," said the posh woman.

"Oh ah? Dun't sound like me."

"You were in extremis at the time."

Judith frowned. "I've never been to Greece."

For some reason, the woman sounded annoyed. "You were calling out to nobody in particular, asking for help. I was watching you, looking for an opening. I took that as my cue to appear and make you an offer."

Judith realised she did remember summat like that. She'd been standing in her kitchen, weeks ago, just after she'd got back from that business with the borders collapsing. She'd been suddenly aware, on the upward wave of the rolling sea of her self-awareness, that she was losing her mind. She'd called out to the higher powers for help. The sort of help that, in her experience, they hardly ever gave. She'd made a wish that her suffering would soon be over. And there before her, suddenly, had been standing Maitland Picton. Judith had known what sort of being she was facing, damn it. She had made deals with devils before. But she'd been such a selfish old woman, hadn't she, that she'd given into her weakness in that moment, had asked what Picton would need of her in return. She remembered the woman's words. "A certain amount of access. A certain amount of control." Judith was pretty sure she would always have said no to that, except then the sea of her self-awareness must have taken her under again, and she had, perhaps, been pliable, been willing to say yes to anything.

Now her hand spasmed, went to her coat pocket. But what was in there? Some internal warning told her not to go there. An internal warning that seemed, literally, to be situated in her guts. She burped loudly and withdrew her hand.

"Tiresome," said Picton.

"Where are we going?" asked Judith, noticing again that it was night and they were walking.

"To wait for noon tomorrow."

"What happens at noon?"

"That is when everyone's wishes will come true."

Autumn's attempts to not panic had failed. She was drawing air in through her nostrils, and a little through her mouth, at a rate that couldn't be doing her any good. But maybe it'd help her think faster. Lizzie, right beside her, might be full of good ideas, but those couldn't help Autumn now. Cramp had set into her limbs, and seemed to be coming and going in waves, each bigger than the last. Autumn vaguely wondered how far pain could actually go before her nerves started shorting out or something. She kind of hoped they did that.

She watched, helplessly, as some teenagers walked past, going into the cricket club fields, playing music loudly from a phone. Suddenly there was something all around her, no, *through* her, what—?

She slowed her breath again as she saw it was another kid, running to catch the others, who'd moved straight through the space she was stuck in. When Picton had said intangible, she'd meant it. It would be too much of a risk to leave them here if someone could feel their presence, even slightly.

It would be easier to bear this if it wasn't for knowing that Lizzie was suffering beside her and that Judith was in that thing's power. There was no rescue coming. She was going to have to do this herself.

She fought down a wave of panic again. Her mind was sobbing but her body couldn't. She was feeling a desperate animal need for help and comfort. None would be coming.

She got control of herself again. That would come in waves too.

What did she have to work with? She couldn't use any spells with physical or verbal components, which left her with the sort of weak-ass stuff which was usually filed under "meditations." Which was kind of like mindfulness, and mindfulness wasn't known for its ability to extricate the mindful one from death traps. Picton really had wanted them to suffer, because she could presumably have set this trap to paralyse them completely, and thus stop them from breathing. Small mercies, eh? Still, she could breathe, so what could she do with that?

She experimented with concentrating on her lips, trying to form specific sounds. No, it was like she'd been to the dentist, only this anaesthetic of her mouth and tongue was triple strength. She couldn't even touch her tongue to the roof of her mouth. Hmm, maybe anaesthetic wasn't the right word, because she was really feeling the blood in her face at the moment, probably some side effect of her muscles being kept at such tension. The pain was getting to that truly scary point now, the point where her body was yelling at her to do something to stop it. A point where she'd never been, at any time in her life. Autumn concentrated on anger, on her need to get out of here so she could get her hands on Picton, could save Judith from whatever Picton had planned for her beyond using her so horribly.

Small breaths, like a spell for lighting small fires, if she could manage some really soft syllables, but no, she really did not want a small fire in front of her face right now. Passers-by might notice it, but then they'd just draw a crowd who'd still be oblivious to them dying in agony. Still, it'd save them from some of the exposure. Maybe she could try that later.

No, wait a second, there was something else she'd read recently, something designed specifically for use by those who couldn't speak, what was—? No, that was no use, that was a spell she'd read up on when looking into cures for Judith's condition. It was something a mystic, dying of natural causes, could use, no matter how weak they were, to . . .

Oh. That was a terrible thought. Reassuring to know she could do that, but . . . but . . . no, wait a second. Spells had rules. Spells were little stories of their own. Spells had boundaries and conditions and perhaps, bloody *per-*

haps, spells also could fall prey to ironic reversals.

Okay, pain again, ride it, wish you could clench your teeth, and there it goes, fading back into what was possibly just, oh, lasting harm. No time to think any more about this then. Let's go for it. So, step one . . .

She concentrated on the correct incantation in her mind, offered up a tiny portion of her strength, and with what tiny air her lungs and mouth could push forward . . . and here came the first terrifying bit of two, sequential, really terrifying bits, the second one even bigger than this first one . . . she blew into the air, really too close to her face, a little flame, which flared and persisted as she screamed internally at how close it was, then found it to be just about okay, and kept on channelling that tiny stream of energy to it, keeping it going.

There were shouts from ahead of her. The teenagers had turned around and were pointing back toward them. This was the scenario she'd imagined, people being puzzled by a flame in the air. *Come on, you lot, show some curiosity, come and . . . that's it, take a video of it on your phone. And you get to tapping on that phone, and yeah, you lot, come closer, come and have a closer look, start telling your friends.*

It took ten minutes or so, of increasingly disturbing pain, before the first adults started to arrive. Autumn couldn't make her eyes move to see who all of them were as they moved around and through the two of them, peering and reaching toward the flame, each seeming to need to find out for themselves if it was hot. She noted them as they went past. There was Chris the young builder, in that beard of his, and Mike who made doors, who seemed to have been out on the beer. She started to have a concussive feeling inside her as the pain burst over her again that felt worryingly like some primal, internal, wobble on the verge of collapse. Should she do it now? Before it was too late? *No, wait, wait for someone . . . someone like that!* It was Annette Manser from the book club, and several other societies, who every year for her grandson's birthday would come into the magic shop mistakenly thinking she'd find a magic trick for him.

Annette was a first responder.

So. Now. While Annette's still looking bemused at the little flame in the air. We're going to bet everything on this, aren't we? But we don't have an option. And if the bet doesn't work, well, it's better than the alternative.

Autumn took all her anger and bravery and a memory of her dad being proud of her and put the incantation into her head that was deliberately easy to say, the incantation she'd found when seeking cures for Judith that allowed a magic-user, on their deathbed, to end themselves. She made herself breathe it out in one soft, terminal breath.

Autumn died.

3

SUDDEN DARKNESS. Autumn was aware of falling. Then of nothing.

Then she heard applause. The applause of centuries.

Then she felt pain in her chest. Then the pain suddenly blossomed to hit her entire body, a spasming of pins and needles that got into her head, too, that made her yell. And cough. And open her eyes.

And there was beloved Annette Manser, a terribly practical expression on her face, pushing down steadily on Autumn's chest. "She's conscious!" she called out.

"But where did she come from?" a voice that sounded like Chris with the beard was yelling.

Autumn tried to get up, but Annette started hushing her, told her to stay put. "We've dialled 999," she said, "an ambulance is on the way."

But Autumn could only look wildly around her, to the space where she knew Lizzie to be. And there she was, invisible to everyone else, but to Autumn a fine set of lines in the air, the same agony on her face.

Autumn shrugged off Annette and stumbled to her

feet, pushing away the many hands which tried to help her. Someone asked if she'd been drinking. She ignored them and reached out for Lizzie. But her hand didn't connect.

But come on, she could do this. She'd saved herself, because it turned out that one of the rules the spell that had caught them was based on was that it was designed to hold living people. She was free and she had to save Lizzie. But how?

This spell must have something to do with moving its victims into another dimension, one attached to this reality, but at one remove. So it was a bit like the divide between Lychford and the other realities on its borders. Judith had once led them on an effort to establish some swift, rough replacement borders around the town. The magic she'd used to do that had been straightforward, had been about associating and pinning, as one might, if one were a completely unethical bitch, associate a potential lover with oneself and pin them to one. And then wait for the hideous karmic consequences, but hopefully not in this case, because, as with the borders, Autumn was going to associate and pin what people mistakenly called "thin air" and soil, not a person.

"Just give me a second to do this!" she yelled, as more concerned people closed in around her. "It's a religious gesture. It'll make me feel calmer." Half of them still thought she was mad. But it had at least given her the few seconds she needed. She managed to make her parched and numb lips mumble the right sounds, remembered what Judith had done with each of the points where they'd re-powered the border, made something like the right gestures, then, in a quick, decisive motion, put both arms around Lizzie and wrote a border around her in the air, annexing wherever she was and declaring it to be part of this world.

Lizzie fell into her arms, yelling in pain.

"The vicar!" someone shouted. "Where did the vicar come from?!"

And then they were all crowding in on them, asking impossible questions. Lizzie looked up into Autumn's face, still terrified, pale with shock. "Come on," said Autumn, "let's get you back home."

Using more power than she had, she managed a single step away from the crowd with her friend and said something over her shoulder that made the crowd confused about where they'd gone, and the two of them stumbled off into the night holding each other up like they were in a three-legged race, their limbs protesting with every step.

Judith stood in the woods, at night, in the freezing cold, looking down at the open grave. Well, it looked like a grave. Whose grave? Hers, probably. She was startled to see a strange woman standing beside it, but then she remembered. The woman had just caused the hole to open up in the ground. The sides were smooth, and the leaves were falling away from it. Judith looked around, wondering where her sister Doreen had got to. There she was, leaning against a tree in her ironic "glamour" pose, one hand on her hip.

Judith laughed. "Where's that lane?"

"Over there," said Doreen, pointing. And sure enough, there it was, over her shoulder, impossibly overlaid on the woods, leading off a little way this time, then still turning a corner, like the entrance to a maze. Down it came the smell of pure winter, of ice and air with nothing in it but frost.

Judith shivered. "That's a real roller coaster, that one. And a maze. I know it's a maze, don't you laugh."

The odd woman stepped between her and Doreen. Which was rude. "What are you talking about? You seem to wander when I'm not propping you up with my power. Oh well, not long to go now." She pointed to the grave. "In you get."

Doreen rolled her eyes and made her "ooh, posh" look.

"Why do you want me in there?" said Judith.

"So you're in the right place for the plan. You'll be nice and warm. We need you alive. Until noon tomorrow."

Judith put a hand to her stomach and felt it turn over again. What had she eaten? "Are you a doctor?"

"Yes, I'm a doctor, do I really have to take control of you again to just make you do this one small thing?" Suddenly, she smiled. "Go on, dear, do it just for me."

Judith wondered, somewhere in the back of her head, if this woman knew how she'd reacted to every medical professional who'd used that tone of voice with her. But still, she supposed she knew best. She remembered that same voice getting her to climb down into a well, of all things. And that had worked out all right. Hadn't it? She supposed it did. She gave Doreen a wink and stepped awkwardly down into the hole, giving a little cry of pain at her hip protesting.

The odd woman moved to help her. "That's it," she said. "Now, lie down, and I'll bury you."

———————

Lizzie sat in an ancient armchair in the Vicarage, her hands around a mug of coffee. It felt like she'd been in hell. She could still feel the ache of it in her. It felt like it would never leave her. "That bitch," she whispered. "I knew she could hurt us. I knew I was right to be afraid of her."

"She played us," said Autumn, pacing. "She came after us specifically, she made a plan and she carried it out." She stopped and squatted down beside Lizzie. She seemed to be trying to stretch the pain out of her muscles. "I'm sorry I let that happen to you."

"You didn't let—!" Lizzie couldn't finish that or she'd start crying, and she was damned if she was going to cry. "We have to get Judith away from her."

"If that would make much difference. Maybe Judith's too far gone already." She talked right over Lizzie starting to protest. "We were her last target. She's moving straight to doing what she came here to do. But what is that?"

"It really is something to do with wishes. She got Judith to lead us off the scent there, so that must be what this is about."

"The wishes the posters asked for, the wishes in those Facebook comments . . ." Autumn got out her phone, sat down beside Lizzie, and found them once again. "All these radicalised wishes. They're all about anger at other people. She's preying on the divisions of this town."

"By stirring up hatred on social media. Wow, maybe she's working for the Russians."

"That would be so much easier."

"But if this is deliberate, that woman who started these comments . . ." Lizzie flicked up to the top. "Meadow Hill."

Autumn quickly found a website about the origins of names. "It's what 'Maitland Picton' means. She didn't bother to conceal that very much."

"But she *did* bother."

"Yeah, so these wishes *are* important."

"And so are the posters. Picton got Judith to put them up. Which is why she could get them into the woods and the well."

Autumn paced for a moment. "Are they maybe being put in a pattern, to make a magical symbol on a map?"

"I don't know. At the Festival meeting, there was something about posters being put in places that annoyed other groups in the town. If the placing of the posters is annoying, some of them will have been taken down by the annoyed. And we've taken one down ourselves. I can't see Picton running about replacing every one that's missing."

"Yeah, it's more like Picton just wanted lots of them out there, more than the Festival committee would have been willing to put up on their usual sites. So this is about critical mass. About having loads of them out there to go off in some way like, I don't know, an enormous bombing raid?"

"She's one of those stick figures, the sort Judith talked about seeing when we first got together. That supermarket chain's plan was about painting signs on people's doors, about singling people out, but it was still a sort of carpet bombing."

"Whatever this is, it's also stopping us from accessing the water from the well in the woods." Autumn got up and paced to and fro. "Like a sort of gravity, like all these posters are concentrating a force which holds it back. That feels like border magic to me, like the water from the well is. Power from out there that's being given to us. So this big lump of border magic that Picton's built up—"

"She said it was going to make our world like hers. In one go. It's a border inversion bomb. Or like . . . have you seen *The Wrath of Khan*?"

"Which one is that?"

"Where they shoot a torpedo at moons and suddenly they're like Earth. That's what she's planning. To change our world into hers."

Autumn took both Lizzie's hands in hers and helped her stand. "We have no idea how it works, we have no idea where she's getting the power to do it from, but we might not have time to find out. We need to find every one of those posters. Before she sets them off."

They left the Vicarage at 4 A.M., bundled up in their warmest coats and scarves, still aching. Or at least Autumn was. She could see the pain etched onto Lizzie's face, making her look older, burdened. And those thoughts took her straight to thinking about Judith. Should she have anticipated the possibility that the old hedge witch might be compromised? Was there anything now that could be done to save her? In Autumn's research she had found charms that could kill, or at least that could reduce to floating cinders whatever that human body was that "Picton" was wearing. But Judith had told them both, at length, about the costs of using magic like that. Magic was like stories, but it was like money too. Effect was paid for by sacrifice, either of oneself or something else, someone else, and if it was the latter, then stealing that power echoed, rebounded, cursed and burdened.

Perhaps that was the responsibility Autumn should take on now? Literally all of human existence might be at stake.

She decided.

As they headed into town, she took a diversion to Witches, ran into her kitchen, pocketed her sharpest slicing knife, and was out again in a moment to tell Lizzie she'd just wanted to grab some protective charms.

If the worst came to the worst, for the world, or, damn it, for Judith, Autumn was just going to cut Maitland Picton's throat.

———————

Judith lay underground. It was dark. It was warm, down here. Well, warmer than it would be outside. Why was she here? The soil smelt nice. It was suspended in a flat surface a couple of inches over her head, and it hung in the air, the scent of a cellar, taking her back to that pub cellar where she'd kissed a barrel delivery man and to the cellar stairs at her parents' house, which was about Christmas, because you went down them to fetch the decorations up. She suddenly felt afraid. Where were her parents? Didn't they know she was here?

But at least Doreen was here; she'd know. She stood in the darkness, with winter light behind her. She was in a different space. She didn't have to fit down here. "Here we are," she said. "This is close to the truth. Won't be long now. Have you got all you need for the journey?"

"Why, where am I going?" But nevertheless, Judith automatically patted her pockets. There was summat sticking in her hip. It was in her pinny, under her coat. She put her hand in and found she was holding a book. What good was that down here? No light to read by. Oh, stupid girl, of course there was. The light of the lane behind Doreen would let her read. Now, if she could just get it out ... She slid it up her body and found there was just enough space to get it in front of her face and slide it open, sideways. That was why she had done that thing, wasn't it? What thing? Oh, yes, she'd arched her back when she'd lain down, given herself an inch or two she wouldn't have otherwise had when she'd relaxed down onto the ground.

Well, that had been an odd thing to do. The rumbling in her stomach had told her to do it. What was that about? What was this book? She smiled when she saw her own handwriting. Oh! These were her stories. About elves—not the elves she'd known, elves when she'd made them up. These words had been where she'd started making stuff up. And she was making still. In this protected book. Another pain from her guts told her not to be satisfied with the start. She needed the ending. Where was the last page? Oh ah, here it were, the new writing, or the old writing, the old *person* writing, because on the last page, her handwriting was spidery and all over the place.

Why had she written a new story? Her stomach rebelled against her again. Or . . . no, it were obeying rather than rebelling, doing what it was supposed to. Whatever that was.

"Is it a good book?" asked Doreen, who had a look on her face that said Judith should just get on with it.

"Oh ah," said Judith. "It's everything I need to know. Just you keep that light on."

"It's not meant to be for you to read by."

"I know what it's *for*. But that's not what it's going to be used for. Not yet."

———————

Lizzie couldn't stop shivering as they marched from noticeboard to noticeboard, in the darkness before dawn. Their only companions were cats, a milkman that waved to them, and the birds starting to shout about territory and power in a chorus that people found light and cheerful and rousing.

She couldn't help but reduce it to what it was. She had darkness in her heart. They ripped and snatched the posters from all the obvious places, but they had no idea what was enough, had no idea where all of them were. Where was Judith? Could she be forced to attack them? If Picton found out they were alive, she might well get Judith to do that. Could they stand against her?

They came to the central noticeboard in the marketplace, the one by the post office that was also a coffee shop. There were lights inside the building, the smell of percolation from within. The noticeboard was locked.

"I think it's a council one," said Autumn, rubbing her gloved fingers together. If they were like Lizzie's, they were numb from pulling and tearing in the cold. They were carrying two shopping bags full of crumpled up posters now. If Autumn had any idea what they were going to do with them, she'd kept it to herself. "You have to get the key from the town hall offices."

Lizzie grabbed her scarf, wrapped it around her hand, and punched the glass. It shattered, and the pieces crashed to the ground. Quickly, she grabbed the poster from the board, crumpled it, and threw it in with the others.

"What the hell?" A cry that was half a shriek came from the other side of the square. There stood Carrie Anne Christopher, frozen in shock, frost scraper in hand, standing by her car, which was parked outside her house on the corner. "Reverend?"

"Run!" whispered Autumn.

"No," said Lizzie. A big and rather scary thought had just come to her. She had a few seconds to mull it over as Carrie Anne came marching toward them, brandishing the scraper.

"Why did you do that?" She went to inspect the noticeboard, as if she literally hadn't believed her eyes, then swung to confront them. "What have you done with our poster?"

"I think you should call 999," said Lizzie. "No, better, call the police station." And she pointed to a phone number on the noticeboard.

It took ten minutes from Shaun Mawson to arrive from down the road. Lizzie breathed a sigh of relief that it wasn't someone from Cirencester, that what Shaun had told her about his schedule, making sure they knew where to find him at any moment of the day for news of Judith, had turned out to be accurate. That ten minutes had consisted of Carrie grilling them about why they'd done it, about why, dear God, they had dozens of her posters in their bags! Had they done something to annoy Lizzie at the meeting? Hadn't she been far enough up the agenda? Was this anything to do with the W.I.? Lizzie had dead batted every question, willing Autumn to not fly off the handle until Shaun got here.

When he did, with a look on his face like he'd suddenly woken up naked at the United Nations, Lizzie turned to Autumn. "Tell him the truth," she said, "about why we did this."

Autumn immediately got where she was coming from. "Shaun," she said, "we're taking down these posters because they're bad magic." Carrie opened her mouth in incredulity. "They're magic so bad that it could mean the end of the world. Today. You know what your mum was involved with all her life. This is to save her as well."

Shaun took a deep breath, then nodded. "All right." He

looked to Carrie. "Whatever these two need to do, let them do it."

Carrie stared. "Are you telling me, officially, as a police officer, that magic is real?"

"Yep."

"So I can call Cirencester cop shop right now and they'll agree with you?"

"I really doubt it. And please don't do that. That would get me sacked."

"So this is just your opinion? That it's okay for—?" She gestured toward the posters.

"Think about it," said Lizzie quickly, seeing the resolute look on Shaun's face and not wanting his bluff to get called. "Is there nothing that's happened to you in this town that didn't make any sense, that you've kind of put to one side because it doesn't fit in with the real world?"

"Well of course there's not—!" And then, just at the moment when Lizzie thought their luck had run out, and that they were about to have to save the world while running from the police and any number of irate local organisations, Carrie Anne Christopher stopped. She looked slowly between them, as if making sure this wasn't a joke. "Show me," she said.

"Look really closely, don't let yourself be distracted," said Autumn. She put the pieces of glass back together in the noticeboard frame, then shoved both her palms at the air in front of it, while making a complex sound in her throat. Lizzie saw the energy flood out of her, saw how much it drained her, left her staggering. The glass was now a single piece again.

"I . . . don't see how you did that." Carrie went to the frame and put her hand on the glass.

Lizzie lent Autumn her arm so she could keep standing. "Worth it," Autumn whispered.

Lizzie could only agree. "Listen," she said to Carrie, "if you believe us, we need to know a few more things about these posters."

———————

They went back to Carrie's house to talk, Shaun as well. Carrie called her work and took a sick day. She sat them down in her lounge without even offering them tea.

"How many did you print?" asked Autumn.

"Well, it was going to be two hundred, but Maitland Picton did a deal with a printer, and we got a thousand for the same price. What? We didn't know they were . . . evil!"

Lizzie had found herself boggling at the idea of a thousand posters in a town with half a dozen noticeboards. "Where are they?"

"They got used up. I thought maybe they'd got out

into all the villages and into Cirencester, but people keep saying they're seeing them in odd places around Lychford. People this year really do seem to know about the Festival."

"That," said Autumn, "is very much looking on the bright side. The non-bright side is that there might not be a recognisable universe left to hold the Festival in."

"You're actually serious. Okay. Okay. They can't all have been put up. Roz has a stockpile of a hundred or so at her house. So does Janet. And I think Victoria has too."

"Why?"

"It's just where Maitland dropped them off."

Lizzie brought up a map on her phone. "Can you point out where those are?" Carrie did so. The three sites formed a neat triangle right in the middle of Lychford. "That's a pattern," she said to Autumn.

"Any three sites form a triangle," said Autumn. "It's more that they're right in the middle, with all the others spread out across the town."

"It's like how you'd dynamite a building," said Shaun. "Big charges in the middle. Lots of smaller ones." They looked at him. He shrugged. "I watch the documentary channels."

Lizzie and Autumn looked at each other. This sounded ominously likely. This, Lizzie thought, was why Maitland Picton had chosen this particular society. The Festival committee were, on average, richer. So they lived in the middle of town. "Is there some sort of . . . deadline, involved with the Festival, before the day itself, some sort of ticking clock?" asked Lizzie.

"Funny you should ask that," said Carrie. "Today's the deadline for our competition on Facebook. You know, tell us what you want to happen and win £20 worth of meat from the butcher."

"What time today?"

"Noon."

"We need to get to those big piles of posters before noon," said Autumn. "And take them far away from the borders."

"What," said Carrie, "you mean into Oxfordshire?"

"We probably can't keep you up to speed on all of this," said Lizzie. "Sorry."

"Our members with the posters all work in London," said Carrie. "They'll have left home already."

"So we break in," said Autumn. "Shaun, have you got some easy police way to do that?"

"Do I look like an anti-terrorist unit?"

"Okay!" Autumn literally ran for the door. "We'll improvise!"

Carrie called the three Festival committee members in question and found that two of them, to Autumn's relief, had hidden keys on their property. They wanted to know what sort of emergency this might be, but Carrie, not having had several months to think about excuses for the impossible, could only blurt that she'd explain later. So they quickly acquired a pile of posters. Autumn ran for the third house while carrying them in a Tesco fibre bag. She realised that she was running weirdly, carefully. She couldn't help it. It felt like she was carrying a real bomb.

The third committee member could not be reached beyond voicemail. Her property, with big hedges and a little driveway, had the light of a burglar alarm blinking over the front door.

"That'll be connected to the main desk," said Shaun. "I'd need to have a major flap on and some seniority on my side for them to deactivate it."

Autumn was considering the prospect of just picking up a rock and smashing the window, when a voice spoke from behind them.

"Okay," it said, "now I'm impressed." They turned together. It was Maitland Picton. She looked puzzled as much as angry. "I left you for dead."

"Oh God," said Carrie. "This is really real." She pointed at Maitland. "This is a formal notification that I will be taking this to a vote of no confidence. You're off the committee."

"Why did you do that?" whispered Lizzie.

"I thought she might, you know, vanish, like a vampire?"

"Because vampires are really worried about getting on the wrong side of Human Resources."

"Where's Judith?" asked Autumn.

"She's being useful."

Autumn saw Shaun react in anger to the idea that Picton had his mother, but she didn't have time to tell him all she knew. Hopefully Picton herself might do that. "So you're not going to villainsplain some more to us?"

"Of course you'd see me as a 'villain.' You've spent thousands of years occupying lands that originally belonged to my people."

"Have you?" asked Carrie, looking to Autumn as if this were something she might be personally responsible for.

"*All* humans have," said Picton. "From the moment this universe of yours suddenly appeared, you've treated the rest of us like you're in charge. Well, no more."

"They're sort of like fairies," said Lizzie. "Only not. Fairies are nicer. Some of them. I said I couldn't keep you up to speed and I still can't, sorry."

"I'm trying to think of something I could arrest her for," said Shaun. "Probably best I can't."

"So we're worrying you, are we?" said Autumn. "We've rattled your cage. What's up? Is there something we can do to stop whatever happens at noon?"

Picton took a step toward her. "I can feel that knife you have in your pocket. It might harm this body, but it can't harm me."

Autumn decided not to look at Lizzie. "It'd be satisfying, though." The fury inside her was keeping the fear under control, and control was what she needed most. She had honestly no idea what she could do to stop whatever Picton was. She was hoping to get some clue to back up her knowledge of the weaknesses of otherworldly beings in general.

Picton was now right in front of her. "I can kill you with a touch. I can bring any existing medical condition within your body to its fullest expression just by putting a hand on your shoulder."

"Good to know. Now you won't get the chance."

Picton seemed to consider it for a moment. Then she turned to Carrie. "Do you remember what you wished for?"

"I . . . didn't wish for anything."

"You did. It was at one of the meetings. I asked you what, if you had a magic wand, you'd most want for the Festival. You said you'd want it to continue after you'd gone."

Carrie's face turned ashen.

"No!" Autumn yelled, seeing what was coming. "We will stop this before noon!"

"Noon was arbitrary," said Picton. She raised a hand in the air. "I'll do it now." And she clicked her fingers.

Carrie suddenly gasped. She staggered. Lizzie grabbed her, holding her up. She looked like she was trying to speak. She fell against Lizzie, then hit the ground.

"Your wish is my command," said Picton.

Shaun ran to Carrie and swiftly began chest compressions. But the look on his face said he didn't hold out much hope. "I am going to arrest you for something," he whispered.

"So it *is* about ironic outcomes for wishes!" said Lizzie.

"It was always going to be," said Picton. "What else would be satisfying? It's about wanting to be tall. It's about wanting the body of a Kardashian. But that's only the start. I'm pleased you're going to try to save her. I like the idea that she's going to suffer for a while. Who knows, you might succeed. There's some hope. Does that make it worse? But on top of all this you're about to have your hands full."

Autumn decided she was going to go for it. Her hand closed on the hilt of the knife and in one movement she swung it hard from her pocket. But in the second it took to get from there to Picton's throat, Picton had vanished.

"Autumn!" yelled Lizzie, concerned not for Picton but for her.

Autumn ignored her, and knelt beside Shaun, who was still working. "I think it's a heart attack," he said. "I've only had first aid basics. Take my radio, call it in, I'll tell you what to say. Let's get the paramedics over here."

"No," said Autumn. "She didn't touch her; this isn't about an existing condition. This is something that was done to her and still is being done to her. It's magic, not medicine. So I can stop it." She took the knife and sliced open her palm. She'd worry about tetanus later. A line of blood added to the pain in her body and made her gasp. "A sacrifice to the east, to the lady and hope," she called out, and threw the blood into the wind in that direction. "All I need to do is heal something tiny that Picton changed. Some blood clot or something." She reached up, found the power she needed had been put into her hands in the air but that a lot of it was going to come from her, really a terrifyingly huge lot of it. She didn't hesitate. She hauled the power down toward Carrie and slammed it into her heart.

Carrie sat straight up, yelling, making Shaun fall back. She grabbed her chest as if Shaun had done something inappropriate.

Autumn fell to the ground. Lizzie put a hand on her shoulder, looking down at her with enormous concern.

And she was right to. Autumn had nothing left. The world was coming to an end, and she'd used up all she had.

"You . . . saved me!" said Carrie. "This is all really real."

But before Autumn could say something about how it was possible that Carrie had had any remaining incredulity, the radio on Shaun's multi-pocketed vest sprang to life.

"Multiple incidents reported," the voice began.

4

CLARE WOODLEY WAS GASPING for air. She'd been about to go into the post office in order to pick up a parcel of what she was pretty sure was going to turn out to be ribbon that she was going to use to make bunting for the stalls at the Festival. But now, suddenly, impossibly, she was looking down at the roof of the post office, and the market square in general, and the early shoppers were ... staring up at her in horror and had started to run.

She took a hesitant, stumbling step away from the building, and found herself swaying on her feet. Why was she so ... tall?

It was ironic, she'd always wanted to be tall. But this—?! She had to call out, she had to call for help. She opened her mouth and tried to make her jumbled brain come out with the right words, but all she could manage was what her increasing, oxygen-starved rage had shoved up into her mind at that moment. "Clare ..." she bellowed, "smash!"

———

Rachel Cobham was in the porch of her home, about to take her son out to school, when she realised that she could hear her husband yelling. No, more than yelling, screaming in fact. She dropped her son's coat and dashed back inside, and was thankful to find him alive and well, but pointing in slack-jawed horror at their dinner table.

Lying on the dinner table was a corpse, its mouth wide open, its eyes staring.

It took a moment of giddy, impossible horror for Rachel to realise she recognised the body.

"Isn't that," she said, not quite believing it even as she forced the words out, "one of the Kardashians?"

———————

Peter Johnston had replied to that Facebook post that asked what people most wished to happen in Lychford. He never replied to posts like that, but it had been early, and he'd woken up with his back aching again, and when he'd let the dog out he'd found those little vials of laughing gas or whatever it was the youths used these days all over his doorstep. So when he'd been looking over what his friends had been saying he'd found that question and he'd felt spurred on by it, and he'd said he never again wanted to see teenagers using drugs in the alley behind his house.

Horribly, he found that was all he could think about now as he tried to desperately keep himself calm, tried to remember where he'd left his phone and find his way to it. He stumbled against the edge of something and fell. He lay on the ground for a moment, hoping against hope that this might be a momentary thing. How could this have happened, when his last eye test had been an all clear?

How could he have suddenly been struck blind?

———————

Logan Shipton and his mates were on their way to school, walking past the park. Brooklyn, who was always talking, was talking now about how he'd figured out the parental access code on his mum's iPad. Logan found himself thinking that they went into that park most nights to hang around, but there was that skate ramp sitting there, like that was what the council or whatever wanted them to do. He owned a scooter, but he wasn't going to take it up on that thing, wearing a helmet or whatever.

Except then, suddenly, he decided he needed to go to it, right now. Around him, his mates were reacting, too, turning to look at the park.

And then they were climbing over the wall, jumping

to the ground, sprinting toward the skate ramp. Logan knew, and the thought scared him, that this wasn't what he wanted, that this was what someone else wanted. What a lot of people wanted. It was now being forced on him. Though none of them had anything to skate with, he and his mates were going to go and play on the skate ramp.

They were going to go and play there forever.

Julia Sturrock opened her door to find her friend Angus, who she always spoke to when they were in the queue at the post office, standing there, looking anguished. "I really have to apologise," he said.

"What for?" She had no idea what he could possibly have done.

"The state of the roads. The potholes. I'm on the town council, you see. So it's my responsibility. And it's just not good enough."

"Well..." Julia had never even thought about potholes.

"Do you forgive me? I'm begging you!"

"Angus, what is this?"

"Please could you just forgive me and let me get on? I've got to do this for everyone in Lychford." He indicated behind him to where Julia, poking her head out of her door, could now see several other elderly councillors, all standing on doorsteps. "We all have."

———————

Luke, at the agricultural college, was listening to one of his fellow lecturers, who had burst into his office and was urgently pointing to his own eyes. "You don't understand," he was saying. "I can see supermarkets paying farmers decent prices for their produce."

"Well, that's . . . good?" said Luke, not getting it at all.

"That's *all* I can see. Everywhere I go. I . . . maybe I went on a bit about this? Does someone think I deserve this?"

———————

Arthur Russell stepped gingerly out onto the narrow balcony in front of the town hall clock. He looked down at the marketplace far below and wished he hadn't. He turned quickly back to look at the enormous clock face. He had in his hand a sponge, and at his feet he'd very carefully placed a bucket of soapy water. He was terrified. He didn't even feel brave. This was so unlike him. All he'd wanted was for *someone* to do something to clean this thing up. He hadn't imagined that he'd suddenly decide that he should be that someone. That was even more un-like him.

He realised he'd seen something strange when he'd looked down at the marketplace, and risked another look. Down there were people he vaguely knew, people like him, *old* people, who were urgently scrubbing at graffiti and futilely trying to push cars off the pavement.

It seemed that everyone who wanted *someone* to do something was doing it. And it was horrible.

Harry Staunton thought he knew why this had been done to him, though he couldn't imagine how the young bastards had done it. He'd woken up with a searing pain in his chest and had almost fallen out of bed. He'd found it then, under his pyjama jacket: a red paper poppy with a plastic centre and stem, the ones that were given out for Remembrance Day, to honour those fallen defending their country. He'd said something on the computer about people being made to wear these all damned year long. Because they were forgetting, damn it, they were turning away from wearing them for fear of offending the people who always got offended.

And so someone had found him and had done this awful thing to him. He was looking at it in the mirror now. The poppy had been fastened to his flesh. The pin went straight through the skin of his chest. It was still hurting like hell. He grabbed one end of it and tried to pull it out. But it wouldn't come. The more he pulled, the more it hurt. He pulled so hard he nearly blacked out. He staggered and fell.

They, whoever they were, couldn't do this to him. They couldn't keep doing this to him. He was going to get it out even if it killed him.

———————

Sheila Coleshill went under a different name on Facebook. She took care not to reveal where she lived or anything about her family. So she could say what she liked. She'd been saying things about the family next door. About how she thought they were travellers who'd been put on the estate by the council. About how she didn't understand some of what they said to each other. About how they played their music too late at night and how their dogs kept barking, and how they seemed to have people around all the time and sat out in their garden and kept looking at her property.

She'd said in that thread that got so many responses that she'd like to see them go to hell.

Now she was standing at her garden fence, still in her dressing gown, weeping. Seeing the adults being dragged into that hole that had opened up, that hadn't been so hard. But seeing what was waiting there for them, through the hole, a vision that had gone beyond anything she had ever imagined in a lifetime of imagining bad things . . . that had been hard. Seeing the kids run and the things burst out of the hole after them and carry them back, gently, like they were prized catches, that had been hard.

Hearing them plead to her for help, finding herself calling to them that she couldn't do anything, that she couldn't move, that all she could do was watch, that had been hard.

The hole had closed. She had thought for some reason that then she might be able to move. But then the hole had opened again, and her neighbours had fled screaming out of it, and through the hole this time she'd seen another hell that went beyond what she'd imagined in an entirely different way, and entirely different things had burst from it and had grabbed the family, and had started to pull them back into the depths of it again.

It was going to keep on going. She knew it was.

It felt like she was the one in hell. It felt like she always had been. And perhaps everyone in Lychford, Sheila realised, alone with their friends in all their different bubbles, had been in it with her. Perhaps hell wasn't other people. Perhaps it was a lack of them.

5

LIZZIE SENSED THE POWER building in the piles of posters in the shopping bags and those concealed somewhere in the house in front of them. She also felt it prickling her from all around, a general sense of it growing, like electricity in the air. It was coming from every poster, she supposed, still attached to every site they hadn't found, all across the town. She looked to Autumn and saw she was feeling it too.

Shaun was helping Carrie to her feet. "I'm not going to be much help," he said. "In a sec they'll send me off to one of these multiple situations." Lizzie had heard from his radio the reports of bizarre things happening all over town.

Autumn had got to her feet but was swaying, exhausted. She'd got out her "detector." "Maybe I can't do anything," she said, "but my tools still can." She let it out of her grasp, still holding the chain, and it sprung out like an arrow, pointing away from the town. "Picton could hide from us while she was in stealth mode," said Autumn, "but now she's summoning all this power to her, now she's about to make her move, her own power is shining like a lighthouse."

"So. We don't have much choice, do we?" said Lizzie. Leaving Shaun and Carrie calling after them, they set off at a run.

————————

Autumn could feel the horror all around her as she ran, and she could feel the horror inside her rising to match it. It didn't feel like they were going to get there in time. And she had no power to do anything even if they did. The power was rising and rising, climbing in pitch. The people they ran past were reeling, some of them beset by whatever awful wish they'd been granted, some of them just staggering with magical potential even the uninitiated could feel. The enormous, concentrated negative emotion was a nonconsensual sacrifice, the power source for whatever vast alteration of reality Picton was about to attempt. Autumn had been right about ironic wish fulfilment being a part of what she was planning. But she hadn't realised that wasn't the end of it.

Now the pendulum of her detector was leading them at a run down to the river, and it was pointing to the wooded hills beyond. Of course. Picton had her engine roaring up to power in the town, and she was going to use it on the borders, right at the point where she could haul on the cords of the bag that was their world, their universe, and pull it inside out, making it into a part of her own. It was an enormous feat of magic. Picton was indeed a professional. She'd anticipated everything they'd done, even that they'd save Carrie before following her.

But she hadn't expected them to survive her trap. She was fallible. She could be outsmarted. Autumn had no idea if or how they could do it again, but they were going to have to try. Together, she and her best friend ran down the path by the river, desperately hoping they were going to be in time to save the world.

———

"Maitland Picton" stood beside Judith's grave, feeling the force gathering in the town below. The sun here, symbol of the ridiculous enormity of the universe beyond, shone irritatingly on her through the trees. So much wasted space. There might even be, in this universe the humans had, whole other nonhuman civilisations out there, whole other *contexts*. And for what? The worlds of magic were otherwise small, otherwise beautiful and original, a cluster of brilliant ideas, inhabited by the creatures of ideas.

Those creatures had regarded this physical

Earth—when it had suddenly erupted, with the expanse of its universe, from out of their own worlds—as a primitive accident. It was surely a side effect of the great transgression, the fall of he who now lay under everything. But it was an offshoot that was interesting enough, that could be colonised. And so the ancestors of those that had made her and others like them had explored here and been seduced, had, as their natures dictated, found themselves attached to the meanings they found here. They had become beings that cared about the moon and the stars and forests and animals, that had ended up continually referring to the minds of the evolving intelligent beings here for reference. The fairies had taken that way too far and gone native, their decadent and corrupt society becoming, well, a commentary on *human* need and nothing more. But when the beings of the original worlds had blinked, time had sped on, and suddenly human minds were a sprawling, threatening, connected, blaspheming, intervening threat.

A disease.

All of the great powers had decided to act, one way or another, even a faction of the fairies. But by then knowledgeable ones had arisen even among the humans, and they had put up borders that used the tremendous incline in energies between their sprawling universe and the original ones to keep out the primal owners of everything. Hence generations of anger in the original worlds. But the leadership of the fairies had shrugged and found ways to hop over the borders and wrote themselves back into human whimsy.

That was what had led to her being assigned here. That was what had led to those like her sneaking their way into the ever-pliable court of fairy and creating a new faction of radicals who longed to be strong like the other original worlds were strong. She'd been told the start of the fairy civil war would be the signal for her to make her way over the borders herself, to begin her mission to end this universe. But she'd shown initiative. She'd felt the borders vanish, rushed to them, seen them resurrected as a shadow of what they had been, and had pushed her way through them.

She stood now waiting for the power to be enough. She would know when, she had been told. It would be like gaining a sense, a limb. It still felt muted, like everything in this world, but the feeling was getting sharper every second.

But now there were shadows moving through the trees toward her. What? They had actually found her. The two remaining guardians, the acolyte who was still trying to grasp the basics and the follower of one solitary path. Well, that was twice they'd surprised her. But now they weren't facing anything that had to hide. She'd brought with her enough power to do this, power made from the willing positive sacrifice of hundreds of minds back in her home, minds that would be unrecognisable to these wretches. She was about to combine that with its opposite—the unwilling negative sacrifice of the hundreds she'd tricked here. Put them together, as she was about to, and she would wield, for one act only, the power of a god.

"Stop!" shouted one of the figures.

"No," said "Maitland Picton."

―――――――――

"I'm scared," Judith said to her mummy. But then she realised Mummy wasn't here. And so she got even more scared. Her sister Doreen was somewhere around, but she wasn't sure where. Judith realised she was holding a book. There was something specific that was making her scared, a rising tide of . . . Oh God, what was this pain she could feel in her chest and shoulder and arm? It hurt like nothing she'd felt before. What was it that she'd said, that she'd wished? For her suffering to be at an end. And thus, it soon would be.

She felt her stomach lurch at the thought of it. And with that lurch came wisdom. Into her head, from where it was being preserved in her gut by the fungus she'd eaten, came the few sentences she'd written into the memory of that fungus. She was once again aware, albeit fleetingly, of everything that was going on. She looked again at her book, illuminated by the light of Doreen's pathway, as she'd known it would be. The book had been hidden in the box, and it had kept that spell of hiding on it while it was in her pocket. As she'd known it would. In it, Judith had written everything she had to do and say.

Maitland Picton had taken advantage of her, had got into her and made her work against her friends. But Judith had prepared a backup. What she was reading now, though, scared her even more. She read that Picton had put her in the ground to be the centrepiece of the sacrifice she'd prepared, to be the sacrifice that set the whole thing off. And this increasing pain meant she was on her way to that, soon.

But sacrifices can work both ways.

Autumn felt the detector make a sudden heave forward, and knew they were close. They rushed into a clearing in the woods, and found Picton standing there, her arms raised, her fingers poised, as if she was about to rip down a curtain. She barely acknowledged their arrival.

Autumn dropped the detector, pulled out the knife, and ran at her.

She hit something in midair that was as hard as a wall and crashed to the ground. She realised, as she hauled herself to her feet, that her nose was bleeding. The side of her face felt badly bruised. Beside her, Lizzie was bellowing prayers, casting out evil. Maitland Picton was laughing at her.

"Just one thing I don't get," Autumn called to the creature, hoping she would, again, want to gloat, that it might buy them some time while she tried to think of something, "why didn't you want Judith to go into Ashdown House? You could have got her out whenever you needed her, couldn't you?"

"What are you even talking about?" The look on Picton's face was one of sighing bemusement that Autumn was still nowhere near being on top of her plan.

But that reaction made Autumn suddenly realise that someone else might be. "Where's Judith?" she said.

Picton took a slight step sideways. Autumn looked past her, and both saw and felt a shape in the soil. She reached out her senses toward it and felt an answering familiarity. Oh God. Oh God. The bitch had buried her. Judith was alive, but she would never recover from this. Autumn made herself ignore that.

She had one tiny hope burning in her now, and that hope was Judith. If it hadn't been part of Picton's plan, why had she used some of her declining power to trick them into not admitting her into Ashdown House? Why had she needed that freedom, that access to her tools, if not to work something? So now Autumn wanted desperately to send some of her own power to help Judith with whatever she was doing. Except she had nothing left to give. Blood was for small tasks. All that she had left in her body wouldn't be enough to contribute much in the face of the power that was building up around Picton.

But . . . there was something she could sacrifice. Something that was valuable enough to her, that was a major enough change to the world, that was close enough to her heart to make a difference. She found the place in her mind that she associated with the points of the compass and the powers that sat outside the circle, beyond the horizon, at those points. She called to them all that she was about to make a sacrifice. "I call to mind my future love, the name of that love is Luke—"

"Autumn, no!" That was Lizzie.

Autumn ignored her. She reached out to the mass of disturbed soil to establish a pathway for the power that would come with sacrifice.

The consciousness in the ground slapped her aside, the pathway broke. There was such familiarity to that feeling. The gesture was so Judith. Autumn started to cry. "You stupid old woman!" she yelled. "Let me help!"

"We only have a few moments left now," said Picton.

"You'd best arrange your afterlives. Although eventually I should think we'll pursue you there too. Ah. Here it comes." And she reached up and grabbed the edge of reality.

———

Judith felt the pain become terminal. Which was a sensation she'd never experienced and knew now only because it was beyond anything she'd known. So she read the words from her book. The words that turned everything she was from a sacrifice someone else was making into a sacrifice she was making deliberately. She sent a quick call of meaning and farewell along the echoes left by the pathway Autumn had opened, that she'd broken, because the girl had been about to throw away her future like Judith had once thrown away hers.

Clever girl. She'd be fine. Everyone was going to be okay, once Judith had made herself do this one little remaining thing. She saw—in her mind's eye, the eye of the wise woman, of the hedge witch—the shape of the worlds, of how the borders to them had been thrown down together at Lychford by accident, to talk, not to fight. The fairies understood that. Well, most of them did. Nobody else bloody had. Well, maybe Autumn. But that was not for her to say now.

In the mental space shared by those who were part of the magic that was happening above her, on the surface, Judith saw the stick figure, the thin twist of information that was Maitland Picton, grabbing at the hem of this world, gathering it into her hands, about to heave on it. She saw hundreds of posters, an explosion of energy, blooming at the heart of Lychford and at dozens of points all around it. The energy rolled toward Picton like a wave, a wave she was about to surf.

Judith mentally moved to be right in front of her. A presence that was suddenly in all Picton's senses. She could sense her apprentice and the cleric as ghosts nearby. They'd barely be aware of what she was doing. Her body was still in the grave. She looked into Picton's stick face, and it was somehow, satisfyingly, startled. Judith grabbed Picton's hands with her own. The weight of what Picton had prepared was falling on them. It had to go somewhere now. It was too huge not to. So, what to do with it? The only move Judith could make would bugger everything up. Would change Lychford forever. But maybe that were for the best. Judith committed herself to the sacrifice. She looked right at Picton and saw the being was scared, saw that she'd thrown everything at what she thought had been the perfect plan, and hadn't seen that she'd overlooked and underestimated an old woman.

"Bye then," said Judith.

She grabbed the universe. She grabbed the tidal wave Picton had set in motion. She threw all her energy into redirecting it, just by a single notch. The woes of Lychford exploded behind her and into her. And she was part of the explosion and was consumed by it.

Autumn staggered under the impact of something enormous. She saw Lizzie falling too. Everything on the floor of the forest lifted into the air around them. Was this it? Was this the end of the world? She looked to Lizzie and they made desperate eye contact. Lizzie reached out and grabbed her hand.

Autumn looked back to Picton. To her amazement, the being was staggering too. More than that, she was yelling in frustration, grappling with something in the air, tottering, trying desperately to hold on as her body vibrated faster and faster, flickering between her human shape and the stick figure that was underneath.

Picton screamed.

The stick figure exploded.

"What?" said Lizzie. "How?"

Autumn knew. "Judith." She couldn't feel anything from the soil ahead of them. Autumn started to climb desperately to her feet. "Judith!"

From somewhere ahead of them, there came the noise of what sounded like a single explosion. Autumn saw, through the trees, through her extra senses, an enormous presence bursting high into the air.

Water. It was water. It was the water, she realised, from the well in the woods, freed from the gravity that had been holding it back. It was like a fountain, reaching to the sky.

A moment later, the first drips of it hit the forest floor around them. Then the downpour began. Autumn felt it invigorating her, filling her with power as it drenched her. Lizzie, beside her, actually started to laugh. And yes, Autumn realised, this was something good, this was something that meant that the world wouldn't end. This was something that was, instead, going to change that world.

But then she started to feel something else, under it, something that was speaking directly to her. Her joy receded, and the dread started to rise up once again.

Across Lychford, the rain thundered down on everyone, as they were flailing to deal with the consequences of the wishes they'd made, as they were struggling to help friends doing the same. Shaun Mawson had got halfway to his second emergency situation when the onslaught of water landed on him, like a bucket from the heavens. Carrie had been trying to convince the paramedics that she felt absolutely fine now, when suddenly they were all soaked. Luke had taken his friend outside, trying to work out what was wrong with him, when the water had fallen onto them. It buffeted his skin, got into his hair, got somehow even further into him.

He looked around, aware, suddenly, that everyone he could see, everyone slowly coming out of the buildings, people who'd been inside, too, they were all feeling the same way he did. He wasn't sure how he was aware of that. People who he was now somehow identifying as the ones who'd made wishes, his friend included, were relaxing, as the weight of those wishes left them, as the consequences were suddenly washed away.

Around him, all of Lychford started to see the world differently. Around him, all of Lychford suddenly realised what they'd been missing all these years.

———————

Autumn was realising something else. She watched, with senses that had become somehow different even from what she'd had before, as the landscape around her rotated, shifting away from the mound of soil under which Judith lay, and centring anew, centring on her.

In her mind, she walked with Judith alongside her, down an urgent path through the trees, hearing the voices of many who'd gone before her. "The wise woman has come to the well. As it has been, as it will be. The hedge witch will take on the burden, and come to the well from the town, and be the voice of the wilderness and the voice of the people."

"No," she said, shaking her head.

Judith put her hand on her shoulder. "It's time."

"I can't. I want to save you. I can't be this. *You're* this. Please don't—"

"You can do this. The world needs you to do it. So stop being such a bloody idiot."

Autumn felt anger rise into her face. "You couldn't just be nice about it, could you? Not even now. I know what sort of life you had, being the wise woman. I know why you were always like this. Can't you understand that I don't want to be like that?"

"Then don't be. I won't get a say in it, will I? Not after today."

"You're not going to give me anything, then? Not a moment of thanks, not a moment of love?"

Judith closed her eyes. "You'll have to make do," she said, very gently, "with what I've already given."

Autumn knew she had a choice. She could step away. She could let the insight that was falling on her shoulders with the rain fall away. She went to Judith and put her hands on her shoulders. Judith opened her eyes. She was calm. Here was all the damage that had been done to her, that she had chosen to take on. Here was a life that had been sacrificed a long time before she had sacrificed it today.

"Yes," said Autumn Blunstone, at last, knowing fully what she was accepting, and yet at the same time knowing and hoping that she would do it differently. "The wise woman has come to the well."

Judith nodded. "Oh ah. You'll be all right." And then, with a flutter of leaves, Judith wasn't there anymore.

Judith stepped off the path and left Autumn back where the young woman couldn't see her. She looked over her shoulder. The soft young thing was shaking, sobbing. But she was already wiping away those tears. Judith looked around for Doreen. She'd been the part of all this that wasn't a hallucination. Ah, there she were. She was standing beside the entrance to that path across and out of the trees, holding out her hand. Judith felt the chill from down that path and shivered.

"Too late to bring a coat," said Doreen. "Here's the truth now."

"About bloody time," said Judith. She didn't hesitate. There was no point. She took Doreen's hand. "Best get on, then." Doreen led her to the path. They stepped into it, and walked back into the depth of the picture, out of the universe, away to summat else, summat old and central that didn't like to make a fuss. Except when it had to. Except when it did.

They got to the corner. Judith hesitated. At the end, she were only human. She looked back to where Autumn was and saw her step away. The last person who could have seen her was gone. "Why's it so cold down there?"

"Dun't have to be," shrugged Doreen. "You never did like the summer."

Judith's old mouth broke open in a smile. And it was a smile that was now, suddenly, a lot easier to make. She took a deep breath and didn't look back again.

She walked around the corner and she was gone.

Epilogue

TWO DAYS BEFORE THE Lychford Festival, Lizzie presided over Judith's funeral. She was amazed at the turnout. Where once Judith had been the sort of individual who'd have got three family members and a single bunch of flowers, now, with the whole town of Lychford aware, albeit sort of distantly, of the sacrifice she'd made, a large number were here to commemorate her life.

"They've woken up," Autumn, all in black, smart as Lizzie had never seen her, whispered to her. "Well, in this one specific way."

Indeed, the life of the town had changed profoundly, though everything remained, on the surface, as it had been. Lizzie and Autumn had been bombarded with questions, as everyone, from the coffee shop proprietors to the regulars down the pubs, had pieced together all that they'd been missing, and had been pleasingly willing to buy them drinks as a result. Everyone in town could now see at least something of the magic around them. They could feel the presence of what remained of the borders, of the well in the woods.

Autumn and Lizzie spent a lot of time warning people not to venture down all the woodland paths the locals hadn't been able to see before but now could. Children especially were being given stern talkings-to about where they were allowed to go. There had been, incredibly, a school assembly about it. Witches was packed with customers seeking advice, information, and protection.

The various town organisations had had emergency meetings, and, usually in one meeting per organisation, had taken their amazement and turned it into practicality. The History Society were asking if they could perhaps advertise their meetings near to this "land of fairy," because perhaps the inhabitants there would be interested. Lizzie had strongly advised against. The W.I. had set up something like a Neighbourhood Watch scheme for the homes on the edge of town. The Festival had scrambled to repair all the ironic reversals Maitland Picton had planted in the heart of the organisation and had done a pretty good job of it. They'd had the help of a town that was pulling together and had heard about how their chair had been one of the first to believe and assist.

The town council had sent out a flier indicating that they really were sorry about the potholes, but they hoped that people had now been adequately reassured of that.

A woman called Sheila Coleshill had been one of many who'd sought Lizzie out. She'd said she hadn't really meant what she'd said as a wish. Then she'd admitted that she had. Then she'd asked if she could possibly be forgiven. Lizzie had told her they all could. That many people in her situation had asked her exactly the same thing. That one old man of her acquaintance had a new lease on life, talking with local youth groups about the importance of Remembrance Sunday and finding exciting new ways to mark it. She'd asked if Sheila Coleshill herself was now talking to her neighbours. Sheila Coleshill had stared at her as if that couldn't possibly have anything to do with their conversation. After a few more words she'd left, and Lizzie hadn't seen her again.

Lizzie had found the first meeting of her churchwardens after the rain to be quite awkward, as it had begun with them staring at her in open-mouthed amazement. What had been a lot easier than expected, however, was taking the body of Judith from where it lay in the woods for a proper burial in the churchyard. That had required a local funeral director who now knew exactly what had been going on (and was a bit worried about some of his back catalogue) and Shaun and Dr. Johnson, who'd been willing to falsify their respective paperwork so that Judith had, seemingly, died at home.

Lizzie kept thinking about the moment they had found her body. Judith had been stiff and cold, her mouth frozen open. Lizzie had seen many dead bodies. Her training had prepared her for this. But this had been different, this had been Judith. Lizzie had kept herself steady, had kept looking into Judith's dead features. She knew that, because people are so used to seeing, without realising it, the tiny signs of life, the slight movements of breathing and pulse, it was easy, every moment, to think one suddenly saw those signs in the dead. It was profoundly odd for those signs not to be there. So one's senses told one's eyes the story that they were. Lizzie's extra senses, though, had confirmed what her training had taught her. She kept expecting, nevertheless, the horror movie moment, for Judith's eyes to suddenly open. The horror movie moment that would be followed immediately, of course, by relief and happiness. The horror movie moment that we all hold in our minds, forever, the edge between life and death. That was what her faith dealt in. That mystery. And here it was. As ever. And as enormous and startling, every time.

After they'd lifted her out of the grave, Lizzie had kissed Judith on the cheek, completely unprofessionally.

Autumn, who'd asked to come with them, had been standing back a few paces, watching, her face set in tension, as if fiercely trying not to cry. But when she'd seen that, she'd run forward quickly and kissed Judith too.

At the funeral, Lizzie delivered an address which was considerably more honest about what Judith had done, and what her life had been like, than she would have been able to be a few days before. She got a bit cosmic about where she believed Judith to be now, about how science, magic, and her own religion all said the same thing to her about a loving father taking Judith home.

Autumn had kept the same poker face until that moment. But then she started to sob, loudly and without reserve, and that set Lizzie off a bit, too, and she had to use all her professionalism to finish.

Finally, Shaun talked about his mother, haltingly, fighting back his own tears. He said he was sure Judith would have been proud to see so many people here. But that she would never have said so.

———

After it was over, and most of those who'd been at the funeral had departed for the wake at the Plough, Lizzie and Autumn returned to the grave. Judith was buried in the corner in the shade of the church tower, where the headstones of the previous wise women of the town were clustered. Her own inscription, at a suggestion from Autumn, affirmed that she'd sacrificed all for others.

Together, they let out a long breath. "Is this going to make our job easier, or harder?" asked Lizzie.

"I think a bit of both," said Autumn. "It's going to be a

lot harder to look after this lot, but at least we'll have their cooperation."

"What's it like, being the wise woman?"

"I don't feel very wise."

"Are you and Luke—?" Lizzie had seen the young man squeeze Autumn's hand during the ceremony, but otherwise he'd kept his distance.

"Judith told me not to be like her."

"Excellent."

"Will you stop having a love life through me by proxy?"

"It's the only fun I get. But, thinking I should get out more, I've decided I'm going to join the Festival committee."

"And I'm going to join the W.I."

Lizzie smiled. "So much for you being the outsider."

"I'm going to do what Judith did, but a bit differently. She did so much. I never knew. I have so many new responsibilities."

"Yeah, we're going to have to do something about the borders. And about whatever's going on with the fairies. Do you reckon we need help?"

"What?"

"If we're a coven, we're going to need a third person."

"You used the C word!"

"I like words to mean things."

Autumn looked off into the distance. "I'd started to think it was really just me, but Judith suffered so much by shouldering all this on her own ... So, yeah. I think maybe someone might just ... present themselves?"

"How do you know that?"

"I'm the wise woman."

"Oh," said Lizzie, "I am going to get so pissed off if you keep on doing that."

And they stood at the grave for a while longer, until they were sure they had both thought of Judith in every way they had to. There would be more visits, and more tears, to come. But they were busy right now. Busy with new life. And Judith would have understood that. Probably.

A few days later, Autumn went to the Lychford Festival with Luke. On a date. Lizzie had smiled at them until Autumn glared at her to stop and she very obviously went off to mingle. Autumn and Luke had several craft ales, and danced to some of the bands, and ate fish and chips from a van, and sat at a table in the autumn night, listening to a DJ from the cricket club playing every magic-themed song he could think of from Little Mix to Take That.

"Yes," sighed Autumn, "I think actually it *could* be

magic. When are they going to get past this?"

"It'll take a while," said Luke. "Everything's changed."

"That'll be the next Take That song."

"I understand so much more about you, now. About why certain things have happened."

Autumn was worried by the look on his face. "Does that scare you?"

"Of course it does. But that's not your fault. It's just the way things are."

Autumn wanted to take his hand. But she still couldn't make herself reach out. "I think I'm right about how magic works. That it's about story, about narrative connections between things not associated in conventional physics. Judith used that to get under Picton's radar. She was the big reversal at the end, the cavalry coming over the hill. Or under the hill. And it took sacrifice, because this is all like money, too, everything she did had to be paid for. Money and story both loom over the world, getting into everything."

"I hope story wins over money."

"Absolutely." That look on his face, Autumn had started to realise, wasn't anything to worry about. It was wonder more than fear, wonder and expectation. As looks went, it was really not too bad at all.

"Did you notice I never came back to ask about that business card? Maybe I should have, in a story."

"You gave me my space. You did better than men do in stories. And I promised to show you what was inside."

"I think you did that for all of us." He reached across the table and kissed her. Autumn dropped her fish and chip fork. She kissed him back. Then she grabbed both his hands, and stood up, and led him away from the table and away from the Festival.

Autumn believed in story. She believed, romantically, that, in the end, some shape to human affairs would overcome chance, and indeed money. That night, above her shop, with Luke in her arms, she moved her own story forward.

And, at least for now, she allowed herself a happy ending.

Or two.

———————

That night, Lizzie woke in the early hours to a strange sound. It was a sound she'd never heard before in her life, one she couldn't identify. She grabbed her robe and made her way slowly and carefully down the stairs, getting more scared with every step. There was a strange, flickering light coming from the kitchen, and the sound was modulating with it, a sort of whine, half organic, half like the wind through pipes.

Last time she'd been in this situation, the intruder had been the fairy prince Finn, annoyed and seeking help. But there hadn't been that light and sound. "Finn?" she called, not managing more than a whisper.

An answer came back, a change in the sound, a sort of cry, but she thought it sounded familiar. Familiar enough, anyway, for her to gain courage and step quickly down the stairs and into the kitchen.

There lay Finn, all right, but there was something terribly wrong. Half his face and half his clothing were burnt away. He was enveloped by the light. Lizzie felt sure that it and the sound were attacking him, somehow. He reached out toward her, his mouth forming the incoherent cry for help she'd heard a moment ago.

Lizzie stepped quickly forward, wanting to help him but not knowing how.

"The court," he shouted, "my father. They're going to bring the war here. You're all going to die!"

"What can I do to help you?" Lizzie shouted over the noise.

"Nothing. Go get the other one. She might—she—" His voice became a strangled cry.

Lizzie was about to run for help. She was about to turn for the door. But before she could move, before she could do anything else—

Finn exploded.

About the Author

© Lou Abercrombie, 2015

PAUL CORNELL is a writer of science fiction and fantasy in prose, comics, and television, one of only two people to be Hugo Award nominated for all three media. A *New York Times* #1 bestselling author, he's written *Doctor Who* for the BBC, *Wolverine* for Marvel, and *Batman and Robin* for DC. He's won the BSFA Award for his short fiction and an Eagle Award for his comics, and he shared in a Writers' Guild Award for his TV work.

TOR·COM

Science fiction. Fantasy. The universe.

And related subjects.

*

More than just a publisher's website, *Tor.com*

is a venue for **original fiction, comics,** and

discussion of the entire field of SF and fantasy,

in all media and from all sources. Visit our site

today — and join the conversation yourself.